. . .

My vision blurs and I am catching myself from falling. We are still together, the procession of us. It is dusk, the sky in the distance is orange and black, the sun is setting behind a mountain, and the air is filled with soot.

. . .

Winner of the 41st International
3-Day Novel Contest

The Loop

by Dan Sanders

ANVIL PRESS • CANADA

Copyright © 2020 by Dan Sanders

All rights reserved. No part of this book may be reproduced by any means without the prior written permission of the publisher, with the exception of brief passages in reviews. Any request for photocopying or other reprographic copying of any part of this book must be directed in writing to Access Copyright: The Canadian Copyright Licensing Agency, One Yonge Street, Suite 800, Toronto, Ontario, Canada, M5E 1E5.

Anvil Press Publishers Inc.
P.O. Box 3008, Station Terminal
Vancouver, B.C. V6B 3X5 CANADA
www.anvilpress.com

Library and Archives Canada Cataloguing in Publication
Title: The loop / by Dan Sanders
Names: Sanders, Dan, 1981- author.
Description: "Winner of the 41st Annual 3-Day Novel Contest".
Identifiers: Canadiana 20200305182 | ISBN 9781772141702 (softcover)
Classification: LCC PS3619.A525 L66 2020 | DDC 813/.6—dc23

Cover design by Derek von Essen
Interior by HeimatHouse
Represented in Canada by Publishers Group Canada
Distributed by Raincoast Books

The publisher gratefully acknowledges the financial assistance of the Canada Council for the Arts, the Canada Book Fund, and the Province of British Columbia through the B.C. Arts Council and the Book Publishing Tax Credit.

We acknowledge the financial support of the Government of Canada through the National Translation Program for Book Publishing for our translation activities.

PRINTED AND BOUND IN CANADA

To Amanda, for helping me escape my loops.

1.

My vision blurs and I am in the forest. I am mid-step and catching myself from falling. I reach to brace myself against a tree, but the tree slides backwards as my arm locks at the shoulder and swings in unison with my left step. My left arm swings with my right step and wrenches the rest of my body violently enough that it forces the air from my lungs. I am walking through the forest. My arms swinging perfectly in time with my steps. It is warm, but not hot and I cannot turn my head. I am walking through the forest. I breathe in on every third step and breathe out on every sixth. I am walking on a path in the forest. I can't seem to open my mouth. I am walking on a path in the forest. I am unable to stop walking on the path in the forest. I try to shake my head, wake up, scream, but my vision blurs and I am in the forest. I am mid-step and catching myself from falling.

The path is painfully exact, a flat plain of undisturbed pine needles, stretching into the distance. A pleasure to walk on and immune to vegetation. Grass grows to its border and stops, each blade bends back, even against the wind, like the path erupted from the earth and made its own space.

It is flawless. The pine needles seem to have been arranged by hand, each at perfect right angles, a bed of x's and squares. I drift between both, seeing only x's then squares, then cubes. I try to make shapes. I have enough control to let my eyes lose focus and fall into the space between the needles. Let myself examine the edges and wonder what it would be like to pick them up with my hands, lay them down myself, and spend eternity making a beautiful, endless pattern, just for me.

There's not a leaf, not an acorn, a pine cone has never rolled onto the path and made little triangular drifts in the pine needles. It is a thick bed, little pricks in my feet to assure me that I am alive, or at least, aware.

As near as I can tell and as far as I am concerned, there is only the forest, there is only this path, I am alone in the forest. I am lost in the pine needles.

I was baptized in a church three times the size of our house. I don't remember my own baptism, but I'd witnessed others as an altar boy. I remember those. They took place in the centre of the church, not by the altar, but fifty feet away, down a long tiled walkway. It was quiet until the baby cried, solemn as a funeral, sparsely attended, and procedural. Very rarely was anyone particularly happy, the baby would be dunked in transmogrified tap water, cry out in panic at being held by a stranger, and the new parents would rush to pull the child back from the priest, back from the water, the expression from all was mostly relief that it was over. A thing accomplished in the centre of a cavernous room — mother, father, child, stranger.

It is just beginning but for all intents and purposes, we are already at the end. The incomplete link between birth and absolution has been completed, an immediate rebirth. It feels tacky somehow to be reborn again so soon, greedy and without consideration for all that's to come. From here on out, the rest is procedural.

I don't remember my own baptism, of course, nobody does. I don't remember much of anything, really, but bits and pieces, here and there, the important parts of my life come through in fits and flashes suddenly and without warning, especially now that I am at the end of it.

It always moved faster and faster as it went, months moving past like days and so on. Everything in life slowly moved further away, pulled across time like a rubber band, and then, in an instant, it suddenly snapped somewhere deep in my chest. The confusion of having to see the distance between now and then as I hurtle towards it, the terror to be able to feel every inch of distance from my birth like it was the slight distance between my limp arm and the glass I've dropped and broken into bits beneath my chair.

I have enough time before I pass to wonder if anyone will find me before the sun moves across the sky again and pulls me from the shade of my umbrella, baking me in front of all I have left, then a moment of relief to finally not feel one way or another about it.

The insects do not cross the hard boundary of the path and never touch me; birds approach overhead and lazily drift away. The path drifts gently to the left, into the distance, as far as there is to see, sometimes uphill, sometimes down. I am allowed to feel the effort. I am allowed to lurch forward and feel the exhaustion of the uphill climbs, and the tricky relief of the downhill passages. I am allowed to feel spry, young, and tired. I am able to feel the joy of remembering these movements. I am allowed to fall and lose my balance, but I am forcibly shunted into posture once I've regained my footing. I must walk. I don't know why; maybe I am dreaming.

In the distance there is a tree large enough that it may have produced all the pine needles on earth. The horizon is generally obscured by growth, but as the tree comes into view, the dense growth fades, like it parted, making way for its king.

This king tree is three hundred feet tall from roots to tip, tall enough that I lose the top of it almost immediately. I lift my chin, but unsuccessfully and I am warped back into posture and forward motion. The tree is as wide as it is tall, a braid of trunks, three trees twisting into one, losing the edges of their individuality as they blend together about fifty feet up, just at the edge of sight. The branches reach in all directions, a giant umbrella of green, veined through with brown branches, the canopy is thick as night, gently weeping pine needles in the breeze.

The need to see the top of it, to see something different, to experience something of my own, grows, and I feel the frustration of my captivity, of my limbs disobeying, of being forced into this shell to walk this path. As I pass close to its base, I force my hand out to touch its perfect brown bark. My fingers almost reach it, can almost feel its presence, the space around the space it occupies, but my arm is twisted, not gently corrected back into place, but wrenched behind me, my shoulder pulled painfully from its socket. I am forced to my knees and held until my vision blurs and I am catching myself from falling. I am walking in the forest and the pine needles have gone.

Our home was a fine but shabby two-bedroom row home in a dense and angry section of Philadelphia. It was small, thin-walled and my mother would eventually tell me the story of how she couldn't keep me from crying – how my crying must have kept the neighbours up nights. She hung extra blankets on the walls and stuffed towels under the door frame to keep the neighbours from hearing, to make it so that she and my father could sleep. She knew that when the neighbours had their kids, they hadn't gone to the trouble and they were up with the neighbour's kids more often than they were up with me. It was a shame, she said, that everyone was so inconsiderate.

I don't remember this either, but I remember her remembering it, calling it up whenever we saw a crying baby, or saw a child requiring more than the requisite amount of attention.

We did most of our outdoor activities at the edge of winter, just before it would become too cold to reasonably swing on a swing set, but cold enough that there were fewer people, fewer children. It must have been November, when November was cold, and the only other child at the playground lost his footing running between the playground equipment. He tripped and fell and split his lip on the sidewalk and cried out. With one hand, she grabbed me by the arm and dragged me back to the car, and with the other, I saw her drive her thumbnail into the flesh of her index finger. It would have bled if we'd parked farther away.

I am walking on a fine brown silt. It gives gently beneath my feet and I learn that I am allowed to cry. The gift of a different sensation overwhelms me. There is a breeze. It is coming from up ahead, instead of off to the left. The trees are smaller. Thinner. Not pines. Deciduous? I don't know what that word means. I feel as though I was walking on the pine needles for years. I know that cannot be true. I am dreaming an endless dream. I will wake up soon. I will be whoever it is that I am, and I will leave this place. The endless woods. Whatever memory this may be. Whatever contorted thing my mind is forcing me to experience. Any moment I will be breathing on my own power. I will blink when I choose. I will be awake. I will not be walking. I will leave this forest. But for now, I am walking alone in the forest and it is relief enough that it is suddenly different.

It has been so long since I have seen a leaf. Crickets. There are crickets here. The eek-eeking, eek-eeking, eek-eeking, drifts in and out as I walk, it gets washed out in the wind as they lift above tall orange grass which whish-whishes in the wind. I dismantle every new sensation into its component parts and weep at the eek-eeking. The newness of the new persistence, doing my best not to notice the repetition of the eek-eeking, the tempo, the exact pause, the whish-whishing of the tall grass feeling intentional, mechanical. The echoes at the end of each noise falling in tempo with my own breathing. Step step step – breathe in eek-eek – step step step – breathe out – whish-whish of the tall grass, blink, eek-eek. My heart drops into the centre of me and would give anything just to take one moment, just a heartbeat break, even if it's here on the path. Just one moment to process, to figure it out, to think but eek-eeking. The eek-eeking. It is the same as it was and I look at branches dancing overhead in their own perfect steps in the steady breathing breeze. Look at the sky, damnit. Rip your head back and look into the sky and feel something yank your hair and shove your head into the ground, breathe in the dirt just to have an unexpected moment and feel your teeth rip the side of your mouth open to bleed into your mouth and puddle around your nose – gasp and snort, and oh god the pressure and then once again into nothing; then, again, the pines.

My father was also a staunch advocate of silence, and

when he couldn't get it, he would settle for predictable noise. When he got home from work he'd turn the radio on immediately. The radio was a large wooden thing set in the corner of our eternally mismatched living room. He'd inherited the radio, it was his father's, or his mother's, he'd told me it'd eventually be willed to me. He didn't know that when he died I would be precluded for legal reasons from receiving anything from whatever was contained in his estate. Though I don't know if he ever properly filled out a will, it's hard to imagine him ever making it to a lawyer's office on any business not related to bail.

The radio only received a few stations and even when it was perfectly tuned it still pulled in a fair bit of static which persisted as a steady undercurrent beneath whatever he was playing to soothe his nerves. I don't think he had any great love of music, or the news, it was white noise, just enough to drown out the sounds of the neighbours, the cars driving by, me and my mother, his own thoughts.

She hummed above it, out of rhythm, tune, or sync of whatever was being piped through the wooden mesh speaker of the radio, which I thought was haunted until I was in my teens. The woodgrain on the side panel hid a demonic face in the knots, in the stain. It was something I'd tried to show them, tried to draw for them: two eyes, teeth, brown and frozen in a perpetual rot of wood. They never saw it, he swatted my head and told me to focus. He always told me to focus, it was his escape out of any father/son moment that lingered past his very short attention span.

She hummed almost constantly. He would ruffle pages. I would watch them for cues on how to do anything other than sit still in a thin film of sound and hope that one of them would say something to the other, or to me, or to comment on whatever noise it was that they thought they were ignoring. It was deafening all the same and I spent most of my time ignoring them, adding another layer of silence, and disappearing into whatever silent activity I could find. I was too young for anything beyond quick picture books, and a TV didn't find its way into the house for another year or two. I remember blocks being a favourite. I remember the blocks were wood but the container was plastic, a big plastic tub with holes cut out in the shapes of the wood. The goal, I guess, was to make a game of cleaning up. So that you didn't leave the red block shaped like the Arc de Triomphe out on the floor for your father to step on at 3 a.m., drunk, on his way to piss or vomit. So that he didn't thunder up the stairs and throw your door open so hard that the handle left a crater behind the quilted wall, almost certainly waking our dear sainted neighbours, screaming and throwing the block at the centre of your chest, the dull thud of it lost in his shouting, your cries lost in your mother's, their fight tumbling out into the hallway, back into the bedroom overwhelming the white noise machine, the neighbours from down the street throwing up their window to shout "shut the fuck up" at the three of us. I think that was the purpose of the little holes in the tub, the general idea, anyway.

One of them threw away the tub the next day. I got to keep the blocks, but the tub was somehow shattered when the fighting made its way to the first floor, to get away from the bedroom windows. It was crunched into plastic shards, underfoot or against the wall, and swept up before I woke up from my padded room to wobble downstairs and look, no tub, no nothing, everything is perfectly normal, let's hum in tempo with news radio.

There were a lot of nights like that – not all of them started because of my blocks, but other small or invisible infractions. It was like we saved up all the noise we were scared to make all week for some weekend outburst, drunken or otherwise. I don't think my mother was a drunk, but she was too careful about everything for me to know one way or another, and she was gone before I really knew what that word meant, or that it applied to my father. I was a child, and my understanding of things was basic and primal. In my mind, my father was a tornado that would sometimes roll through the house and it was best to stay out of his way at all times, just to cut the odds of being in the way when he was spiralled up and tearing things apart.

I think it would have been helpful for her, in the long run, if she'd taken a path like my father did, and I eventually did, to shut out all the noise with something useful: drinking. Drinking at least, in the moment, feels productive. It's an active participation in the world and an investment in yourself. It was like hanging quilts all around your insides. It had the same basic effect. Whatever you're trying to silence builds up inside you all the same, but shouting or weeping or anger or violence is more civil when you're drunk, it's forgivable. You can't run around your life shouting and weeping all the time. You drink to get it out of your system. You don't let it take hold of your abdomen and fester there, releasing itself in one grand final moment at the Jersey Shore. You get rid of it in bits and pieces over time, as penance for being.

She took walks, which sounds healthy, but mostly I think she walked and ruminated, worked over her days and planned her escape with her fists clenched or didn't do any of that and pretended that everything was just fine, which would be worse. I distinctly remember hearing her tell someone that my father "doesn't have a drinking problem, he just likes his drink." His drink. He liked drinking so much that the very concept of drink belonged to him, but, even still, in her mind, he did not have a drinking problem. It was just all forced out of her mind. Not even out of sight, very much in-sight, but still very much out of mind.

She worked at the local hospital, in the emergency room. She was a medical tech, not a nurse, she had just enough training to be involved but not enough to do anything about anything, not enough to feel responsible in any way whatsoever, just enough to be nearby, participate as our family participated best, as a witness.

She worked a lot of late nights and seeing tragedy after tragedy must have inured her against the very idea of tragedy, worn her down over time, made her own experiences seem normal. At least, at home nobody was bleeding, generally speaking.

On the rare nights that the three of us were all seated around the kitchen table that barely fit in our kitchen, and the even rarer nights that he was coherent enough or hungover enough to have a passable conversation about the daily activities of the other people who lived in his house, and the even still rarer nights when the idea to ask her about her day flitted through his idiot head, she'd giggle as she told stories about the horrible things she'd seen. She'd go on about the people who'd been in accidents, or in car wrecks, bodies tangled and compressed, burnt or broken in misery and pain, and how she ushered them from room to room, humming all the way.

She'd lay it all out for us. Maybe it was the only way she could hold my father's attention, which in its rarity became intoxicating. Or maybe it was to protect me from the rest of the outside world being as dangerous and violent a place as it is, but she would get into deep detail about the positions of people's insides that had spilled out over whatever outside, and just roll her eyes about

"What do people expect? I mean, what did they think was going to happen?" at whatever it was that happened.

I had nightmares about the car accidents she described and the occasional spot of blood she'd bring home on her scrubs. I was young, but old enough, trained well enough about the horrors of existence, to know that something terrible happened out there to everyone and all we could do was laugh about it, understand that it was something that happened to people who were not careful, then put it through the wash, and forget about it as quickly as possible.

This was life. You are careful and you forget about it and you make as little noise as humanly possible and just maybe it'll turn out okay, or maybe you'll be infected by the allure of it and spend too much of your life rolling around in all it had to offer and you'd take too little caution and wind up a spot on a nurse's pant leg, a cautionary tale she told her family to keep them protected but also at arm's length. "You should have seen this guy's head, it was a complete mess. Just wide open. You could have rested your drink in his brain. Drinking and driving, the idiot. I know you like your drink, and you can do whatever you want, but you be careful unless you want to turn your head into a coaster."

She would say these things frankly, matter of fact, performatively undisturbed in her confidence that the world was not a particularly good place, and it mattered very little, considering that she was certain that she was going to heaven.

In the distance, beyond the leaping crickets, there is a mountain, high, snow-capped, grey blue. I lose ten degrees of heat just looking at it. I can feel the mountain already, immediately. I know that the path leads to the mountain in the same way that I know that there is only the path. There is no end. There is walking on the path or there is pain and darkness.

I am walking alone in the woods and my mouth is still full of blood. I may have lost a tooth when whatever it is that has my strings forced my face into the dirt. I cannot search my own mouth with my own tongue. I am walking alone in the woods and I am punished with pain and darkness whenever I forget.

My father's only attempt at sobriety was a nightmare almost on par with his drinking. I was eight, it was a year before she died. I remember a lot of it, he remembered all of it, and took every opportunity to remind me of it. He was sober for one summer. He'd been brought home again, not in cuffs, but brought home by the cops all the same. The next morning, he woke up with an incredible hangover on the couch, naked apart from a T-shirt. He had a gash that ran left to right across his forehead that would heal into a jagged, white scar that would never fade.

He would tell me later "Alan, we're talking about an all-timer of a hangover." That it was before he really understood hangovers, knew how to deal with them, knew to drink a pot of coffee, carefully prepare a small glass of hot mustard and pickle relish, drink it quickly and, most importantly, chase it with an ice-cold beer. This would defeat the hangover, and knowing that then would have kept him from holding a bag of frozen peas on his head, taking shower after shower, and finally deciding to get sober and give being a human being one good go.

"What an idiot I was." He was.

That was May of my eighth year. In June, school was out for the summer and so far he'd been unable to handle being at work sober, being anywhere sober, he didn't know what to do with his hands, didn't know where to sit, how to behave. At dinner in early June, he turned up the radio and finally heard the static that pervaded through every station. He took it apart, removed the insides as though he knew how a radio worked, "How hard could it be?" But only succeeded in pulling the wires into a bird's nest, into a thing that would have likely caught fire if he plugged it in, so he left it alone, broken and dead in the corner of the room to fixate on for the rest of his life. "Maybe I'll turn it into a bar, or a fish tank, I want to do something with it, or maybe I should finally have someone come out and look it over, take it apart, find out what's wrong with it, and get it going again. Or maybe I'll turn it into a bar, or a fishtank."

His relentless puttering during those months was matched only by my mother's, who occupied the room directly opposite his for the entirety of the experience. He was in the kitchen, she was in the living room, or the basement, or anywhere else. He was in a sort of mania, now that he'd stopped constantly ingesting a depressing liquid. It happens. It happened to me every time I tried to quit. I heard it described as letting go of a beach ball under the surface of the water. All that time spent underneath the surface builds up, and when it's finally released, it rockets out of the water and into the air before settling back on the surface. We both could never make the journey back to the surface. We'd hit our peak and then figure we'd been healed, free of the demon for good, and so we'd get back to drinking to show our dominion over it and would only succeed in strapping weights to the beach ball, dooming it to sink deeper beneath the waves. It happens. It's part of the process, ups and downs, on and on forever, amen.

The peak of his attempted recovery happened in late June, three weeks of sobriety that he experienced as a full summer. "We should go camping. Why have we never gone camping?" Camping was in his head somewhere as a father son activity, a wife activity he guessed, if she wanted to come along and watch the boys be boys. He got excited and ran out to Sears and bought a bunch of camping stuff with money we absolutely didn't have, and we loaded up his barely functional Buick and we went north to Pine Creek Campground, in June, without a plan and without having reserved a spot, which someone older than eight should have known would present some problems.

We arrived, just barely, in his Buick. The full weight of the idea settled around my father's shoulders about thirty minutes into the dead silent drive. Each of us staring at the road, my father smoking cigarettes through a small slit in the window that focused and sharpened the wind into a screech that shot directly into the back seat, where I played with one of those puzzles where you slide the images around a square full of squares with one missing. Eight pieces arranged just so would reveal the image of a grey-blue mountain, the peak of it cracking through the clouds.

I spent most of the drive lost in the puzzle, falling through the face of it, enjoying the escape for as long as I could. The drive was only two hours, but it was clearly wearing on them both to be so near to each other for so long. We took too many breaks to stretch our legs, got gas for the car twice, and the two-hour drive grew into four. We arrived later than we'd planned, the ranger station was already closed, and all the campsites taken, so we slept in the car on the side of the road on top of all the new camping supplies.

In the morning, my mom finagled us a spot while my dad paced in the parking lot and smoked cigarette after cigarette, flicking the butts into the underbrush.

We squeezed between two campsites, too close for anyone's comfort and apologized profusely for the hassle. My mother was vibrating at the idea that we were putting anyone out, bothering anyone in any way, while my father just shouted at me to hurry up, help him set up the tent, *no not like that, not that way*, as though either of us had ever set up a tent. Finally, as the day got hotter and the tent was still not set up, the fishing poles still in the car, my puzzle solved and scrambled and solved again, he snapped, shouted at the both of us to get away, go away, he'd do it himself. It may have been ironic, because my mother and I had been sitting at a picnic table not helping, but we walked away all the same. My mother went in the direction of the gift shop and the ranger station, and I went the other way. I don't know which way. Just away, along a path, with my puzzle.

I was lost until well after nightfall. Cold and thirsty and bored of my puzzle. It went on forever in all directions. Every so often, I'd hear my father's voice, or my mothers, or a stranger, off in the distance, too far away to really know which direction it was coming from, and I'd pivot on my heel and walk in that direction until I heard another sound, either a voice, or the snap of a twig, the crunch of a pine cone or the rustle of the bushes, that would send me fleeing in the opposite direction.

It got darker, and darker, and I only had my ears to navigate by and I wasn't very good at it. I just crunched my way through the clearest path for hours, never really stopping, panicked, until I felt the ground beneath my feet change, harden, scrape my sneakers in a distinct and familiar and wonderful way.

I was able to flag down the next set of headlights. I'd somehow wandered into a road and thankfully the next person who came along wasn't a drunk or a kidnapper or my parents. I wailed into this stranger's chest, dirty, scraped, and bug bitten from walking directly through thickets for seven hours, my head pounding from dehydration, mouth completely dry. My very first hangover there at the age of eight.

When I was returned to my parents my father made a familiar lurch towards me, he looked loose, uneasy on his legs, a fellow camper had offered him a flask to take the edge off his distress, and he'd taken it gladly. I foolishly reached out for him, assuming I'd be picked up and comforted, but he slapped me clear across the face, the heel of his hand connected harder than the rest, and I went down in a heap. I hadn't yet gotten anything to drink, and the blood pooled in the space between my lips and gums and I never forgot the sensation of returning to consciousness with the wet warmth of my blood rehydrating my dry and cracked bottom lip. I cried harder, panicked, and would have run straight back into the woods, but my head wasn't there, I was woozy and barely hanging on.

My mother picked me up despite my being too big at this point to pick up comfortably, she let my feet drag between her legs as she hauled me back to camp, where she kept my father mostly quiet and entirely away from me, but repeating to me variations of, "Well, what did you expect would happen?" and "How could you do this? We had to call for help, firefighters." She was holding me, but shaking, teeth chattering, staring off into the woods.

It didn't seem to occur to anyone that it was a mistake, that I'd gotten lost by accident because I was eight, had never been in the woods before, and that I hadn't gotten lost at anyone. I just lost my way.

We left the next morning without the camping equipment, left the tent standing and the lantern on the picnic table, but my father kept the flask. My mother drove us home, my father and I slept off our respective hangovers and we made it home in a shade under an hour and a half, and separated the moment we entered the house. My father to the living room, me to my room, my mother downstairs and out the back door for a long walk.

There is a grain of sand in my eye and I am allowed to feel the scratch of it, see the prism of its body glint across my vision as my eyes close. I play a game with it, try to pass it back and forth on each blink. Every thirty seconds, try to enjoy it, try to find it, try to move it with my mind, just for anything to focus on but the path, but it doesn't move. It stays on a rail — up and down — with every blink, sending glints of colour through my brain every thirty seconds. It is a scratchy nightmare and it disappears the moment I feel thankful for it. It is removed from my eye and suddenly I am catching myself from falling in a narrow blue hallway.

My footsteps echo. There is woodgrain panelling on both walls and the hallway stretches blue and brown into infinity. There are cheap fluorescent bulbs under plastic diffusers. Office lighting. I am in a suit and tie somehow and I am unnaturally cold. The air conditioning is on too high. The sounds of the insects are gone and it is just the hum of the lights, the thrum of the air conditioning vents, the swish of my polyester pants. The smell of the carpet cleaner is too powerful, a cloying perfume, trapped in an endless, windowless corridor.

You wouldn't notice it unless, like me, you've been

walking for weeks, months maybe. Walking is automatic. A miraculous series of complex movements, ground smooth by age, repetition, experience. What started as a teetering series of dangers, winds up being effortless, a triumph of evolution and persistence and parenting. People get so used to it, so bored by it, they run and jump, flex their muscles against all of gravity, disregard the ingenuity of each joint moving in synchrony with the rest of your body. Every inch of you bending, flexing, lifting to give yourself over to gravity for just a moment before catching yourself on the other end only to do it over again, over and over again. You might not notice that your gait widened for a split second, just enough time to move your body imperceptibly to the left a few inches over the course of a few steps, enough to make room in the hallway for another person. But I did. We do.

In the hallway I am joined by another. I believe it is a man, I cannot turn to see him, we walk in lockstep together, each movement mimicked and measured and exact. We double the sound in the hallway with the swish of our polyester pants echoing down the hallway into forever. It must be a man because it smells like a man. He also smells like only recently he'd been thrown in the dirt.

We walk for ages. For longer than I have ever been awake in one stretch. We get no closer to any end, the hallway only bends as the path always bends slightly to the left into the horizon. My mouth has time to heal. The bleeding has stopped, the taste of copper has cleared, a distant memory, the smell of dirt has left us both, and now there is only the smell of the carpet cleaner and the purified air conditioning.

It is maddening. I am losing my mind. I will wake up soon. Out there, beyond this, I must be asleep, entombed in blankets, blissfully unaware that any of this has taken place. This is a nightmare. I would have woken up from a nightmare, but I must be so comfortable. My legs, now, in this place, are exhausted. I did not know there could be exhaustion, but there has been no rest. This has been the longest stretch without punishment, without darkness, that there has only been the press forward, through this hallway, hopefully to some end. Whatever end. However it ends, please let it end. For the love of god please wake up.

My partner lunges forward in a fit, a man after all. I recognize the jerky motion of it, he is resisting his movements, he is breaking away. He is not being punished. Maybe there is freedom after all. Maybe there is control. Maybe we can escape together. Maybe he can save me.

He gets ten feet before he is suddenly airborne, picked up by some invisible hand and twisted, mangled and thrown down mid-step next to me. He is urged into movement and jerky, forced steps. He resists, makes a sound like a scream, that grows, and sustains into gurgles, into language, into: "Never ends." And he is broken in half, folded down, and pressed into the floor, his body shatters, dries into fine yellow sand, and is left in a pile behind me.

I move three feet to the right over the course of twelve steps and my heart feels like it will explode out of my chest. I walk for another hour or so vibrating in panic before my vision blurs and I am catching myself from falling on a beautiful sandy beach.

Everything went back to normal after the camping trip, the routine of it was comforting. And I know from my own battles with sobriety that my father was relieved to get back to normal. I know that he felt the loss of the alcohol every second after the mania passed. I've heard of that never fading, some lucky souls get up and over the waves and never come back down, something about their brains has been irrevocably changed for the better, they say. Something about the process of being a drunk and then getting sober has altered the very chemistry of their souls and they are all the better for it.

I never believed them, or anyone, and always assumed that sober people are liars. Or maybe they were in such a spate of panic that they simply couldn't believe it, unable to process the pure fear of having lost all that they'd known to this point, the safe comfort of going to work, getting fired, going to a bar, coming home stumbling, and screaming at your family until the sun comes over the horizon, or finding themselves in a different place altogether, having blacked out and simply become somewhere else.

That panic, the panic of being in a place you hadn't travelled to, of simply and suddenly waking in a new scenario is profound. I imagine that is the state those poor sober souls trap themselves in, unaware that they are not hovering above the waves, but skating on thin ice, perpetually stunned to find themselves in whatever situation they have slid into, having never planned to exist soberly in the world, with all its demands, all the pressures, all the banality and the never-ending nature of everything. It was more sensible, I thought, to allow yourself to ignore whatever it is inside you that tells you that something else is better, that some other part of you is being drowned beneath the waves, and instead know that you are the water, you are the weight, there is no beach ball, there is no breathless escape.

I know that now and my father knew it then. He had his three months of sobriety and he saw what it did to him and he saw the opportunity to blame his lack of sobriety on his child for the rest of his life, and he took it. He decided the stress of his child almost dying of dehydration in a very thin wood just outside of New Jersey was reason enough to give in. I was the perfect and eternal reason for everything that I could later accuse him of ruining – my childhood, etcetera. And even if he was wrong, even if I wasn't the actual problem, I still was. There's no difference between reality and fantasy in this scenario, if he says I was the cause, and he believes it, I was the cause. I am the cause. I will be the cause.

"Everything was going fine until you took your constitutional in the goddamn wilderness." Then when she killed herself, he was set, he blamed me for him, he blamed him for her, I blamed them for me. He was on his path, and I was on mine, and we'd collide together spectacularly down the line somewhere, and that was just fine. Let's try to ignore it, it's easier than pretending that we're meant to do anything else other than destroy each other and those around us.

I do not catch myself from falling. I am permitted to fall completely. I feel my hands go into the sand. I taste it in my mouth. I am not held or thrown, I am operating under my own gravity. For just a moment. I am being given a view of the beach, I am allowed to turn and look as my companions are sprayed to life by the mist, materializing as they stumble, hands first, into the yellow sand.

One woman catches her palm on a seashell and she instinctively reacts, holds her hand to her mouth to clean the wound before she is ambulatory, her arms locked at her shoulders, she is walking, her hand spraying drops of blood for the others to follow, whisked down the beach in procession. As they pass, I join them, ushered toward the back.

I begin to count the sunrises somewhere in the second week of the beach. It begins to feel like the beginning. Like this was the destination, this massive group of us, walking for weeks in pairs. We have climbed mountains and meandered through abandoned cities, walked through high tide, gasping for air on every third step, eyes burning from the salt. We are a team. Sometimes the people in front of me are miles away, sometimes I am nearly stepping on the heels of the man in front of me. He is bald. If I could move my arms, or close my eyes, I could draw the freckles on his head with my eyes closed. Little red constellations that fade in and out as his sunburn raises and fades like the evening.

I noticed the sunburn was healing a few weeks ago. Once red, I thought, his flesh will burn off his skull over time. I don't burn as easily. I am darker, have thick hair. I have no freckles. His skin is permitted to burn for four days, then it resets, on and on. I watch it get darker and darker until he is almost purple, and then it is gone. I don't know if he is healed, or if, in that moment, blink of an eye, we are allowed to rest somewhere else, somewhere other than here, and we are not permitted to experience it. Maybe my bald companion gets a week off somewhere to rest, recline, and mend his wounded skin. I hope so. I hope he enjoys it. He is probably a nice man. I hope he is a nice man. I hope I am a nice man.

Between the time of the camping trip and my mother's disappearance, nothing much is different at home, but there's a distinct feeling of detachment. Each of us has begun the process of phoning it in that will last all three of us the rest of our lives. We have each mentally vacated the family in a way that felt new, like a deeper commitment to avoid each other had taken hold.

We'd never really been that into it in the first place, a series of complicated mistakes and Christian principles had led to my creation and their marriage and it'd sustained mostly because of that indifference and those Christian principles, but somewhere between the woods and home we'd all given up. All three of us had checked out mentally and it was really wonderful. It was the best nine months or so of my childhood.

It was still stressful and bleak, my father still came home drunk, from wherever it was that he went, he would smash things from time to time, but it had no counterweight. Nobody cared that he'd smashed whatever he smashed. His filth became part of the experience of living in our shabby home. The blue carpet that had greyed over time had taken a stark turn into the browns as he'd wandered into the house with his boots on, never bothering to take them off. The couch that did not match the loveseat came apart on one side when he'd come home in a fit and jumped over the arm of the chair, stretching out completely and belly flopping into the squeak of the springs and bringing the base of it down to the floor. It'd never be replaced; it would linger in that spot for years until I dragged it out the front door one weekend when I was sixteen and every bit as drunk as he was.

It had no effect. All of his moods just bounced around our thin walls, and my mother, who'd barely left her room as it was, really committed to her confinement. She'd retreated fully to her bedroom to read novels or sleep for every moment she was not at work or walking around the neighbourhood. I barely saw her before the end. He was allowed to continue apace, and we all watched dumbstruck as the wheels of this experiment began to fall off.

We are walking down a four-lane highway, all the cars have parted to either side, driverless and dusty. There is a commotion ahead. The drop of it reverberates through the line of us, and in the distance I see partners separate and rejoin, a river going around a rock. When it is our turn to move out of the way, we are allowed to look down on the woman who cut her hand on the seashell, our leader as far as I knew.

She is being pressed into the hot asphalt, her legs are at unnatural angles, and the asphalt begins creeping up her sides as we pass. Blood is pouring from her mouth like a river, she is being bound to the road, the ripples across her dress leave the impression of a hand — an invisible hand after all — pressing this woman into the pitch, allowing her to scream, allowing us to hear it. She is passing through it almost unimpeded, maybe through the earth, maybe to hell.

I have not been punished since the group of us came together, since the time I was shoved in the dirt and lost a tooth. I have learned my lesson. I did not need to be told twice. I believe that I am the kind of person who understands things quickly, who is sure to wake up any moment, who will have plenty of time to scream and resist and walk in different directions when this is all over, once I've done exactly what I'm meant to and once this is all over, it will likely be any day now. Any moment.

The bald man is reduced to rubble in front of me. He dries up as he walks. His scalp is allowed to melt off his head over time, and then he is, in an instant, dried out and crumbled as we walk through a tulip patch. His parts combine with this perfect dirt, these perfect little dirt clods, the kinds little boys would throw at each other and come home filthy. He is reduced to those dirt clods after he tried to jump into a river from a red bridge.

I feel like I lost a brother and mourn him for months. His replacement has nondescript brown hair that is frozen in place, does not move, is not unique or interesting in any way. It looks exactly what I assume the back of my head looks like.

We went to church every Sunday, but after the woods my father stopped going. The ruse had been revealed and he'd resigned himself to being the neighbourhood drunk and my eternal adversary. My mother continued to attend, continued to force me to attend, to try to force some of the spirituality that governed her very-difficult-to-rationalize life. She used it as a cudgel to beat her life into a shape that she could live with, temporarily. Until the woods, when it felt that it'd maybe sprung free from its shape, having revealed her son to be a depressive wanderer like her, and revealed her husband to be more violent and beyond compassion than she had ever thought. She understood a lack of compassion, she shuffled her way through a revolving door of tragedy night after night, and had allowed it to wear down her original intentions to a bare, just-following-orders minimum. She was inside the hospital and what happened to these sorry souls happened out there in the world, a large and busy place she wanted no part of.

At first, I assume, she went into service as a religious process. She couldn't be a nun, she'd been careless once and had a son, but she would have enjoyed the regimented existence of the convent, the daily prayer, the constant and purposeful judgement, the tutting. Oh, the tutting she would have enjoyed, scoffing at the rest of us, being a nun was to be a professional at saying "What did you think was going to happen?" Order and proper form, not making a sound, blending into the background, and frowning at the very idea of everything. She fit the mold of other nuns I'd known over the years, but my father had ruined it, if it had been in her mind. It was hard to know what was in her mind. My father too. All three of us, completely inscrutable to the others.

The hospital was the next best thing to a church, it suited her. Order and routine spoiled by the chaos and the mess of humanity. If only they'd come here first to be saved, then we wouldn't have to save them. Think, idiots, why don't you think, what did you expect was going to happen?

I could imagine her entering the profession at the beginning with the sincere desire to be helpful, to help others, to give her life to her fellow man, and I'd only visited her a few times to see her in action. The final time, I remember seeing a large bald man sitting with perfect posture, trying not to touch his gauze eyepatch, which was dotted red with blood. He was sitting bolt upright, not tied to anything, not a gurney or a wheelchair, just sitting on a regular plastic emergency room bench like the rest of us. The only open seat was next to him, so I sat and he reached out to me, maybe not knowing that he was doing it, and my mother exploded around the counter and slapped him on the side of his bleeding head. She shouted "Don't you touch him," then wrenched my arm around my back and took me out to the parking lot, threw me in the back of my father's Buick and calmly told my father "take him home, never bring him here. Neither of you should ever come here again. Not ever."

That was probably six months before it was done. By then she probably knew what was next, she probably knew how it was going to go, she knew that she was essentially leaving me in the back of that Buick forever. But she straightened herself, went back to work, and my dad drove me home, told me to go to bed. He went out drinking and she didn't come home for two days. When she arrived home, she said something about working a double, but neither of us pushed her on the details. He'd only gotten home a few hours before she did and was too hungover to bother with any of it.

We are in pastureland. The sun has stopped rising. It has been a pre-dawn pasture for months. Maybe too many of us have been counting sunrises; we are always kept off balance, or I am, anyway. Maybe everyone else is just fine. There are sudden shifts to new environments, quick changes of pace. Sometimes we are forced to run. We feel our lungs and are allowed to crumple in exhaustion, or clip our toes on tree roots and tumble over hard gravel. We are permitted trips and falls, cuts and bruises. I think someone died without the influence of the hand. It seems unlikely, but someone seemed to have a good old fashioned heart attack. She looked so peaceful. I couldn't believe how jealous I was. How much I envied her escape. Someone broke the rules. Someone beat the system.

Dozens of others are ripped from the line, launched into the sky or compressed into the earth. I am content with waiting my turn. I don't rush it. I am fine. The consistency of the path is my only constant. No matter the environment, I can always count on the path. A slender thirty-degree bend, visible on climbs and descents, my only true companion. The relentless march forward to somewhere. I believe that I am going somewhere, that I am here for a reason, and I will arrive safely to the end of this journey.

I had no idea if they were coming home, assumed they weren't, and if I'd been older, would have been fine with it. But at eight, it was harder, I was dependent, alone, and afraid to leave the house after what had happened in the woods. A ranger said that continuously wandering only serves to make you more lost, and that you should plant yourself in place and call for help. So I did. I sat on the couch and called the bars and the hospitals and asked for my parents, but nobody had seen them. So I waited it out. I sat still. I watched the television and the door and tried to ignore my nerves.

After that night, after being home alone for two days at the end of summer, with the normalcy of the school year approaching, my parents came home after a two-day mostly unexplained absence. I thought maybe they were doing it to prove a point, this is what it feels like to not know where your family is, this is what it's like to panic and feel terrified you'll never see them again, to balance the scales of their wandering through the woods in the darkness calling out my name. I gathered the courage to ask them, "Is this because I got lost?" and I watched their faces become completely confused by the question and felt my heart go over the falls when I realized that it hadn't occurred to them. They hadn't thought of it, hadn't realized I'd been home alone, had not known that their counterpart was equally undependable and had assumed I'd be fine, or worse, hadn't thought of me in two days like I'd died somewhere in the woods and was no longer their concern.

My mother said no, and got sad, then panicked at the answer, and my father, already reclined on the couch, covered his eyes with the crook of his elbow, waved his other arm at me, like I was being ridiculous. "You're fine. Grow up. Focus."

I think they were doing it to punish me, subconsciously. I learned a lot about the subconscious in prison. Leaving me alone wasn't intended, but it was enacted. Or maybe only she was acting that way. I don't know. I don't know if he had a subconscious, or was only subconscious. He moved from moment to moment reacting to whatever happened to be in front of him. He was like a raccoon.

My vision blurs and I am catching myself from falling. We are still together, the procession of us. It is dusk, the sky in the distance is orange and black, the sun is setting behind a mountain, and the air is filled with soot.

We are at the edge of a treeline, halfway up a mountain, taking the thirty-degree bend of the path upwards, around the circumference of the mountain, towards the fire on the peak. Maybe it is a volcano. Maybe it is a live volcano. Maybe the march has been to this volcano all along. Maybe I will be thrown into a live volcano as some sacrifice to whatever keeps throwing us into the sky.

Not knowing has been its own formless concern. Not having control is freeing, life as a waterslide. I go in the direction that I am pointed, and there's simply nothing I can do about it. I can't turn around and walk in the other direction, I'd be ripped to shreds. This is the only world that I have. Maybe in my blinks, I meet up with the bald man at his day spa, and he recovers from his sunburn while I am granted the capacity to understand. Maybe I am told my name. Maybe I am given enough of myself back that I understand what it is that I am missing or what I have done to deserve this.

Maybe I am not given anything at all before I am thrown into a volcano. But probably not. There is only the path, there is only walking in this direction, there is the sound behind us, driving us forward, the threat of death and the absolute silence. There is the shift of my vision and the catching myself from falling. This is all that there is.

The volcano soot makes it nearly impossible to breathe. I dutifully take my gasps every few steps, but it is poison, it feels familiar, I am lightheaded and dizzy. There are lights in my eyes so bright that I almost don't realize what I am seeing.

There is a man, silhouetted in the smoke, walking in the opposite direction, the opposite direction, the opposite direction, directly away from the fire, away from the gas, not in a line, not forward at a slight thirty-degree bend, but in the opposite direction, on his own power, walking casually down the rocky slope.

He is wearing the same clothes he was wearing when he died, when he was put in the back of the ambulance, when they took him to the hospital, and put me in handcuffs. He looks healthy, but confused. There is still blood on his shirt from the impact, but he still has that fucking stupid moustache. As he walks past me, we lock eyes and he smiles. I manage to scream before I am punished with darkness and my vision blurs and I am walking alone in a forest, my bare feet crunching over the pine needles.

2.

In my thirties, long after she is dead, long after my father and I should have stopped speaking, I fell into a routine of meeting my father for breakfast. It was a Sunday ritual neither of us were able to escape. We were almost always hungover, eggs and coffee were always medicinal and burdened with impossible expectations. Surely these eggs will cure us.

He was older and had gotten better over the years at hiding his hangovers, pretending that the pulsing redness was just on his side of his eyes, and not radiating out through burst capillaries in his face, the blooms on his nose. His mottled and weak grey complexion that should have set in twenty years from now is the result of weary age and the result of the world on his shoulders. He sometimes managed to seem grizzled from the effort of a good life and all the drinking he did to cope with that effort, and less like the drowning man he was ten or twenty years ago. Or maybe it's the drugs. I never knew for sure, but it seemed like he may have been knocking something else back with his coffee, papa's little helpers. It could have been some professional drinker's concoction before breakfast, something with horseradish or coffee, something bar adjacent that upped his energy for the hour we met. Some crutch to help him keep his head just above mine. Some edge to grind me on. It's difficult to know for sure, he was impossible to know for sure.

We met for breakfast and, at the very least, tried to punish our hangovers with coffee and unpleasant company. We went to the same diner every Sunday. We knew to meet at ten, even though we agreed always to meet at nine, and at the end of each and every breakfast we would say "Same time next week?" and the other would say, "Yeah, let's make it nine next time. I have a lot to do next weekend." Neither of us ever had anything to do.

Dad hadn't had anything to do since mom died and I never had anything to do just in general.

At this point, we were both still living in a small section of a large and angry east coast city called Philadelphia. I always hated it there, but everyone hates it there. The people who love it, only love it to make you hate it more. Philadelphia is adversarial. My father loved Philadelphia, would wince at the idea of leaving it, ever since I'd ruined the mountains, and my mother ruined the shore.

We settled on this diner because my dad loved the pancakes. They were exactly the same as all other pancakes on earth, but he swore they were different, better, and that maybe he was cursed with this knowledge. Maybe he was the ultimate pancake prophet, doomed to know that the best pancakes on earth were at this shithole diner that was seemingly always filled with eleven hungover people, thirteen if you include the staff.

I was cursed in other, non-pancake ways, including the curse of being the kind of person who believed in curses. I shared that with my father, another superstitious dope. My mother must have also; she must have thought we were being punished or plagued by some devil-sent demons, forced to live out every one of our mistakes over and over. We could have rallied around this point, if we'd thought to. It would have been nice for us to settle on the idea that we were somehow not at fault for the way we were, instead just locked into motion through some unknown force, to show up and eat eggs every Sunday after suddenly finding ourselves outside of the egg place, after waking up hungover, after drinking the night to bits, after swearing we'd never drink again.

I hated this diner. I once saw a waitress throw up behind the counter and nobody even moved. Nobody was shocked, or was unable to eat from the familiar smell, nobody checked to see if she was okay, it was just part of the charm here at Lucy's. *Lucy's Diner — we're all going to die, so what difference does it make.* We just kept drinking coffee, kept pounding back the pancakes, kept looking out the window and not across the table.

We never knew anyone's name, despite spending nearly ten years of Sundays there with the same crew, every Sunday. Pam, maybe. I think there may have been a Pam. But it was the same waitresses, the same customers. There was a man at the counter who read a newspaper and drank his coffee and fluttered his paper back into shape. You could set your watch to it. He was fun to watch when my dad gave his pancake sermon, or started talking about how the neighbourhood was going to shit. We'd found a place to be among other people who all seemed to share a similar disinterest of getting to know anyone else in the room. It felt like home.

I never tried the pancakes, just to drive him crazy.

My father would talk at length about the pancakes and none of the other customers would chime in, but he will mention the changing neighbourhood, or the government and sometimes you'll get a "hear, hear!" from counter man, or an appreciative "Don't I know it" tsk from our waitress. Beth? I think her name was Beth. When she smiled you could count her teeth, she had thin grey skin, and was a nebulous age, somewhere between twenty-five and fifty. I think she was in recovery and it maybe wasn't going so well. When I saw her I'd think, "Maybe my father should be in recovery. Maybe I should be in recovery." Before brushing it away with "I am just hungover. I get depressed when I am hungover."

The days after a long night were filled with regrets. I learned over time that it's a physical condition. It didn't have anything to do with me or anything I'd done, it was just a temporary chemical imbalance from the alcohol. The beach ball. At this point I'd still believed in the beach ball. I just needed coffee. I'd be fine if I could drink enough coffee. On particularly bad days, like this one, I might try a few Gatorades. I couldn't afford to have a two-day hangover this week, I'd tell myself every week. Too much to do at work, or finding and applying for work.

My father, the piece of shit, would find a quiet moment to smile at me over the pancakes to let me know he saw it, saw my wheels turning, saw the panic blossoming. He could always tell what kind of shape I was in and I could never tell what kind of shape he was in. He was a master at making you hate him. Every bite of breakfast became adversarial after a while, and to be honest, it took hold pretty quickly after my mother died.

I should probably explain what happened to my mother.

Mom stole my Dad's Buick and drove to Ocean City, New Jersey to a condo she'd rented from a friend. We'd been there before, it belonged to a friend of hers who we never met, who she refused to talk about. The very top floor had a view of the ocean, over the telephone wires, over the Flamingo Motel across the street, over the boardwalk out to the ocean.

Ocean City is a dry town, and I think she liked that it drove my dad crazy to stay there, to have to pre-plan his alcohol consumption, to spend the entire vacation counting the bottles as he drank them. I think she thought it would make him more aware of his drinking, but it didn't. He mostly slept on the couch.

The Jersey Shore was a nightmare, a condensed Philadelphia. Surging, furious, chaotic, and loud in the summer, but up high, with the wind kicking off the ocean, it would all get cut away. It was loud and quiet, like we liked it. You could breathe up there, scream if you needed to.

The porch on that rental was as good as it was ever going to get.

She'd rented the condo for a week, but as near as we could tell, she was only there a few hours. She drank a bottle of wine, then she slit her wrists and threw herself over the balcony railing.

At the diner, my dad would make jokes about how she must have wanted to be sure. She "must have really, really wanted to go." He'd ham it up. She died when I was nine, about six months after the incident in the woods. He was polite enough to wait until I was ten to start making these jokes, and then he made them almost constantly either to convince me that her death didn't bother him, or to convince himself, though both ideas were the same to him, I think.

I always thought the blood must've scared her and that was why she jumped. Not the sight of it, she was used to blood, or for fear for her life, which she didn't enjoy, but for the carpet.

She was meticulous, afraid to be a bother, and an endless, fidgety cleaner. She couldn't sit still either, so I imagine waiting for the blood to leak its way out of her arms was too much to bear. I assume that even then she was humming, watching it for a few seconds, then got impatient and nervous and jumped to be done with it.

She never hummed any song in particular, just the kind of loose and flat humming that goes on forever in every direction. *Dah dah dah. Do do do. Hmm hmm hmm.* When she worked nights, she cleaned all day before my father got home. Then when his car pulled up, she'd hustle downstairs and out of sight and he'd notice or he wouldn't but the house would be spotless because it drove both of them crazy if it wasn't, then she would leave out the back door for her shift at the hospital. In good stretches, they wouldn't see each other for weeks, but her shifts were fluid, and when she worked days, it meant the house would be crowded with the three of us and pregnant with the expectation of shared experiences. Meals and television, how was your day, don't you have any homework, can you get me a beer, etcetera.

She wasn't afraid of him exactly, she wasn't weak, but she was remarkably polite. She didn't like him very much and didn't know what else to do about it. If you don't have anything nice to say, etcetera.

Her religion kept her chained to him, and by proxy, me, though I don't think she liked me very much either. She had her endless routine spelled out for her, it was going to be the end of September soon, and we'd go to the shore and she'd pretend to want to be there and what was the point of any of it anymore.

I loved her, I guess, but I often wondered about how we'd have gotten along if she'd stuck around. I never found any spirituality, which might have been a plus, considering the conclusions she came to, but I also turned out to be much more like my father than either of us would like. I thought about her in quiet moments for the rest of my life, and like my father, I mostly thought of her in relation to me. How she would have viewed my life, how she would have helped or hindered it, I never thought about her own trajectory. Whether she would have worked at the hospital forever, if she could have found another life instead, if she could have learned magic tricks or Spanish guitar, if she would have stuck around and let her life go in any direction, if it was even possible for it to have gone any other way than the way it was going.

It was easier to not have those thoughts and think instead about whether or not she would have liked my apartment, if she would have approved of the choices I have made or didn't make. It was better to deal in the finite and known elements of my own experiences and sprinkle her into the places she wouldn't make things any worse. She would have loved my apartment. She would have hated my boss. She would have done things the same way that I did things and what better armour to have than a dead mother who approved of her handsome and good boy and who certainly didn't kill herself at the notion of accidentally creating another one just like him.

The cleaning gave her something to do. A way for her to productively occupy space in our lives, while we sat, dead but alive, in front of the television, not talking to her, or each other, because we were busy sitting and feeling uncomfortable in our skin, in our house, with the only other two people who knew us and didn't like us very much any more than we liked ourselves.

I think of my mother doing that calculus as her blood left her body. That some other wife, trapped in the highest floor of this castle, would have to scrub her blood out of the carpets on her hands and knees, and I think she hummed pleasantly as can be as she went over the railing like a scuba diver. I think she was excited to have done something so nice for everyone. I think she was finally free. It does surprise me that she didn't think to put plastic down, like the quilts on the walls. I think that would have solved all the problems, so I think in the end, she just got too excited to waste another minute preparing and just went for it.

My father would say, *She was always fucking nuts.* Every week, we tried to not talk about my mother until we talked about my mother. Her death made a cul-de-sac in my father's brain. He would make the same few statements, talk about the same few things. He would talk about my mother before he talked about the pancakes, he would talk about the pancakes before he talked about the economy, before he talked about society, before he talked about the changing neighbourhood, and just after he'd exhausted all his anger and his bile, he'd take a sip of his coffee and look out the window and get wistful, and then he'd go back to his pancakes. She was still in there, in his head, trying to clean.

My father's paths of conversation always went downhill.

Everything was awful. Sometimes he caught himself saying anything in particular that was positive: the pancakes, the Phillies were having a good year, the stock market was finally picking back up. But he was physically incapable of not mentioning the other diner, with the shit pancakes, the Phillies years of winless drought, the fact that he didn't have any money in the stock market anyway so what did it matter.

He was poor. Me too. My career was a series of failures. I think his forties were surprisingly good to him. After we'd collected my mother and put her back in the ground, his life started to turn around. Having that anchor point of negative energy taking up so much of his life, it caused the opposite reaction in him, he was forced to pump positives into the air. Sure the Phils were bad, but it's not like the time my wife hated me so much she cut her wrists and jumped off a building. So there's that, at least. Suddenly it's a rebuilding year for the Phillies, rather than an elaborate conspiracy perpetrated by Major League Baseball against the people of Philadelphia. "The Wild Card race was fucking rigged," he shouted at least once a year at the diner. The echoes of my mother by then were fading and he'd long since returned to his miserable centre, the beach ball floating on black water.

He was awful in large part because he was born in this neighbourhood where everyone was awful. I was awful also, my son, awful. My father's parents were awful, abusive and drunk. I imagine them gaunt and tall, dressed in grey clothes beating him in the corner of their sparse wooden home that I have constructed from movie and television scenes from a time before urban sprawl.

Our neighbourhood was a black hole and it was nearly impossible to escape. I can't think of any other reason why. Even after I left, I was never free of it. I would catch myself thinking things I knew I shouldn't, doing things I knew I shouldn't, shouting things in diners I knew I shouldn't. A lot of people would blame the drinking but I think it's bred into us, a hereditary dissatisfaction, some broken mood-regulating gene. I never figured out why that is. I was always too hungover to worry about things I couldn't fix.

"How's the job?" My father was exclusively worried about my ability to hold down a steady job, and even when it was going well, he'd suggest that it was soon to fall apart. He was always right, but I never knew if the mention of my failure was enough to instigate my failure, enough of an excuse for me to wade into and wallow in my failure.

The focus on my life and my career, if you could call it that, drove me crazy, but it was not out of line. I couldn't hold a steady job. I told myself I mostly didn't care to, and would forget all the times I would have panic attacks in otherwise calm buildings. The idea of being around others, working for them, meeting, or exceeding expectations would drive me to small, dark corners of impossibly fluorescent structures to breathe heavily into clasped hands and wait for the shaking to pass.

I think he thought I drank too much, even more than he did, but I deflected and told him that's only part of it, that the drinking was the fault of the job, and not the other way around. The real reason for all the failure was the general level of misery radiating from the centre of my chest out into the world at a perfect arc, a beam of darkness created by that fractured gene, or the lousy neighbourhood, or by him and my mother. He had it too, though he never admitted it, just to drive me crazy, but it was there in both of us. He was depression, she was anxiety, I was both.

We were miserable people, doomed to dislike everything that didn't reinforce our belief that we were supposed to be sad, and doomed even more to bring the things that make us sad into our grasp as quickly as possible to use as a bottle opener.

"It's fine," I say. "My boss is a fucking idiot."

"They're always idiots."

When my father agreed with me, it made my eyes water, and I typically wouldn't hear the next few words out of his mouth. There was a rush like I can't believe and I wished always that it weren't there. I wished that the feeling of being in sync with this hateful old drunk didn't give me a rare flood of positive emotions, blurring my vision, and giving me one second of joy, but it did. Even then. I am thirty-two years old at the time of this batch of pancakes, and his constant negativity still created a need in me to hear him say anything positive, some vague approval, just one 'atta boy.'

With lack of direction, I found myself settling for restating his hatreds and agreeing with almost everything he said just for something to say, nodding my pounding head while he talked. I also hated who he hated, I also hated the things he hated. I didn't realize this was all he was. When I tried to impress him, tried to trick him into an atta boy, he'd ask me if I was kissing his ass, or tell me that what I did was not that difficult compared to the hardships he'd faced, that kids my age were all the same, always wanted some handout, never willing to work the way he had, somehow forgetting that he very rarely worked.

When I was a kid, the only constant before and after my mother died was that I mostly did everything wrong and my father really loved forcefully pointing it out to me, his hand on the back of my neck, or his hand wrapping around my scrawny bicep. Leading me to whatever mistake, whichever oversight or stain on the carpet that caught his eye and led him spiralling into sputtering.

I wanted so badly to be Greg Smith's son. The Smith brothers were as unremarkable as me in every way, except their father really seemed to like them and enjoy their company. Even now, years later, I think that was our only difference, apart from the drinking.

I was the same age as Miles. Jesse was a year older, Doug a year younger. Greg was the same age as my dad, but seemed twenty years younger, vibrant and alive. He smiled when he saw you. My dad hated him, thought Greg's natural inclination to kindness was some scheme to steal from our family, sell us something we didn't need. Greg was a school teacher in the next town over. "It's a longer commute, but what kid wants to go to school with their dad?" My father would tell me, "If I taught at your school, I'd fix it so you'd get straight A's. Sit you next to the prettiest girls in class. Greg is screwing those kids over so he can look high and mighty."

We all attended the same Sunday mass in the days my father could still be bothered to go. Greg was the dad who sat up front, sang the loudest and was, according to my father, a terrible person in disguise. My dad would say Greg was a fraud, that you should watch out for those who draw attention to themselves, and that Greg probably cheated on his wife, or helped the priests collect little boys, and it was years before I knew what that meant, and years after that until I realized that wasn't true. He was just nice. Greg was just a nice man.

I lost track of the Smith brothers. I found one of them on Facebook while I was drunk and low but never reached out. His profile image was of him and his wife and three kids, all in the kind of clothes you'd buy at a fancy hiking store. He also grew into the spitting image of his father and I don't want to bother him with a friend request and remind him that I exist, my face making him remember my father's, our faces so old for our age, and that trickle of thoughts made me think about myself as I relate to my father all the more. I looked at my veiny hands, the wispy hair on my arms, up to my chest, which I somehow always expected to fill in with a manly pelt of hair, but never did. I took off my clothes and looked in the mirror, drunk and weeping, and counting the freckles on my thighs, becoming lost in the pattern, and knowing that my father probably had the same number, the same constellation of blotchy dots on his sternum that may have been an early sign of liver trouble to come. I imagined his in full bloom, working outwards from his torso, an explosion of muddy brown radiating from his centre like a diseased firework.

This was the first time I truly considered killing myself. Drunk and naked in the bathroom, unable to control myself, heaving into a 3 a.m. panic attack that was set into motion by having a passing thought of a nice man I once knew.

I woke up in my bed, not remembering how I got there. I was alive but not relieved, having decided to leave the scissors in the bathtub and my laptop in the toilet.

I called my boss, exhausted, hungover, depressed, etcetera, and quit. "Hi, is this Gary? Hi Gary, I quit. Goodbye forever, Gary." It was the polite thing to do, knowing that I'd never go back to that particular job ever again, especially now that I was pretty sure I wasn't going to kill myself, despite the lingering idea that it would be a very funny thing to do to my father. "I thought about how you and I were similar, so I killed myself so there'd be less of you." Would have made a great suicide note. I practiced writing it out on paper on the back of an envelope. I re-read it and all the silly energy of having done something so ridiculous and funny drained out of me and I threw it away, then dug it out of the trash, lit the corner of it with a stove burner, and tossed it in a pan to burn. When it needed help, I relit it on the burner, then remembering I had vodka in the freezer, lit it en flambé, and took the bottle back to the living room and let the letter crinkle to ash in the frying pan, while I got to work getting back to level.

I enjoyed drinking and I did not enjoy other people or my family or the place that I lived most of my life. I thought it was important to do what you enjoy as much as you are able because you never knew when you might cut your wrists and jump off a building. Life is short and too short to do anything but exactly the things you like to do, and to stay away from other people who would keep you from doing these things. Even it if it means your only interaction with others is asking them to lift their legs while you vacuum under their bodies or being collected by them after blacking out on a beach in the dead of winter. I might not have had a career, but nobody bothered me when I needed to burn cursed objects on the stove and use the experience to pretend I was so rattled by the idea of having written a suicide note I needed alcohol to calm my nerves like some Civil War field surgeon. This was not traditional success, but my life was how I wanted it to be in that exact moment, and that was still a victory worth celebrating with freezer vodka.

My father hated vodka, said it was a drink for queers, and so I drank it all the time to spite him — my freezer had three or four bottles at any given time. It never froze completely, but when chilled as far as it could go, it barely had a flavour. You could almost pretend it was water. A miracle all for me, to spend the day in safety, wrapped in blankets watching the television while my first suicide note smoldered on the stove. It was not traditional success, the way most people would understand it, but it was good enough for me. A victory of retreat. If my father barged in right now and saw the state of the apartment, smelled the treacle of plastic window envelope melting into adhesion with my only non-stick pan, he'd roll his eyes until he saw the vodka bottles and then he'd have a violent fit about how I was a failure.

I don't think my father actually ever gave too much thought to how a person succeeds — or if he would have considered a life free of others a complete success — but he understood that it was important that a person did succeed. He stole from his employers his whole life. My father never held a job for long, he hated it in the same way that I always hated it. The difference was I tactfully and quietly withdrew once I decided that it was time to leave a job, politely stopping showing up to work, my father usually got caught stealing or sleeping or found a reason to punch out his boss if nobody caught him stealing or sleeping.

At the diner the following Sunday, I braced for one of his most common conversational detours: "Work is the most important thing a man can do." I figured I'd have to tell him about the quitting, I'd omit that I'd gotten drunk and full of dread about turning into him, examining myself in the mirror, and almost killing myself with scissors. I feel like he probably already knew those things anyway, would be able to read it in my face, and would be happy about it. I often thought he was controlling my actions, especially those that I couldn't really account for once I'd become clear headed again.

I got lucky. He walked in with a black eye and whenever he arrived to breakfast visibly wounded, or limping or holding his ribs, I knew that we'd at least be on even footing. Once he healed, he'd make up for lost time and we'd return to focusing on my life's various failures and he'd double down and make a scene, maybe throw coffee on me. But a bright and swollen eye meant he couldn't get after me too much. I caught him up on my latest quitting, and he took a long time telling me that he'd gotten beaten up by a concrete contractor he found himself working for. He told me that he gave as good as he got, that the concrete contractor was half his age, and was probably still in the hospital, "which is what he deserved for sneaking up behind me like he did, attacking me out of nowhere." He told the story as he flaked grey chips out from under his nails that had yellowed and were dying from the concrete lye or his liver or whatever else. "He got what he deserved, so I won't be going back even though they're making a mess of the job. I could fix it but fuck 'em."

Work had not beaten him, a man had, and that man was an idiot who didn't know what he knew about concrete, despite having never worked with concrete in his life. "People are idiots, but I'll find something else. Work is the most important thing a man can do."

"Yeah, I'm not sure about that."

"Well, you're wrong. You don't know shit."

He always bounced from job to job. After mom died, he went back to working at a mailroom under the El, Philadelphia's neglected elevated train system. It was the third time he'd worked there. The mailroom changed hands several times. It was a difficult business full of large machines that were impossible to sell or physically remove from a building, so owners would cycle in and out and my father would submit a resume, stating factually, that he'd worked in mailrooms for several years, but omitting that he'd worked several times in this particular mailroom, and that he'd been fired twice for stealing mail.

Nothing of value is processed through a mail room. My father would come home with reams of paper and boxes of envelopes. "We'll never buy another envelope for as long as we live." We stored the envelopes in our damp basement next to a ten-pound sack of salt he'd stolen when he worked at the restaurant supply store. We mostly ordered out and I would bet he had 10,000 envelopes until the day he died.

He knew I knew all these things. He knew that I knew that he was not a great provider, certainly no Greg Smith. Money came through our house unevenly, in fits and bursts, and I wore clothes that were too small for me my entire childhood, which he used as an excuse to call me fat.

My mother was a medical technician at the hospital and brought home a regular pay cheque that sustained us and he spent whatever was left over. Once she was gone we were adrift, left to live on his wits. I was nine and panic became part of my body, something I didn't realize was there until I was much older, after I understood that it was there, that it was never leaving, and the best I could do was learn to tune it out.

When he was home he was drinking — never enough to ever call the police or anything, he wasn't overly abusive or violent, he was just drunk and puttering around the house. This left me to do whatever it was that I wanted to do, which was mostly to try and not remind him that I required attention. When I did, he would snap and scream and I would hide and start over the next day, more quietly this time, more self-reliant and alone.

At my mother's funeral, I knew instinctively that I was to function as a sort of emissary to my father. I was to guard him from interference, and I was to allow him to sit in a funeral home folding chair with his head in his hands, and watch his tears drip past his dangling tie. At the time, I was amazed he had so much emotion about it. I didn't know he liked my mother. I knew she didn't like us. I knew I didn't like them. After a while I figured he was holding his head due to the effort it was taking him to file her death into his excuse drawer. It would allow him to wallow and focus his energy on drinking and the more people saw the sadness, the more he could later abuse those people, who would instinctively assume that this sadness was genuine and a cause for kindness. He was masterful. Before he died, he borrowed money from half the people in that room and never repaid any of them.

When people approached, I was to act as receiving line and apology centre – I am an amazing apologizer. One of the best. I was to make sure that people knew that I knew that it was going to get better. It was important for someone to be able to function at this social gathering that people really seemed to be enjoying while my mother was in a box just to the right of my equally unresponsive – except for the weeping – father. There I was alone again with the both of them. I didn't even know who any of these people were. Dozens of people I'd never seen before filed in through the door. I knew my aunt and my uncle and their spouses and my rat-shit cousins and that was it. Everyone else was brand new, I assumed they were there from the church? I never paid enough attention. I was always head-down at church, but now I was heads up, he was heads down. It became a show, a place for people to gather and bear witness to Grief and the Magical Handshaking Boy.

"Thank you for coming, I am nine, my father is not seeing people right now. I am nine years old, thank you for coming, he's not feeling well right now, I will send him your best wishes, yes, hi, nine. No, he's going to need a few minutes." And on it went. I had no grandparents. They'd died before I was born, my mother and father had one sibling a piece, but none of them were on good terms, so the three of us operated as cohabiting only children before she died. Until my father woke me at 4 a.m., alcohol on his breath, shaking me by the shoulders, pushing me into the bed, letting the bed springs shove me off the surface, bouncing me back to life. "We found her. She's dead. Alan! We found her! She's dead. Alan. We found her." He kept shoving me down. He lost himself in the movement. I am awake and floating through the air, and I better take care of Dad, he seems like he's in bad shape.

Hi. Thank you for coming. My father needs a moment. My mother's name was Elizabeth, she was six feet tall, and tried her best to never look me in the eye.

The older I got, the more I understood them both, and the more it made me want to watch television while lying on my side, drunk and wrapped in blankets, heating my house with suicide notes until I wrote one that felt just right.

I lived on the first floor of an apartment building, and it was my only option but it was still a mistake. It always felt like a temporary hold until I lived in my car, or under a bridge without the weight of possessions, sweltering in the heat but beautifully alone. I didn't know that prison was coming, but it was, and whatever happened, I knew even then that I deserved whatever happened next. A childhood of churchgoing made me believe that life balanced itself out and punished the appropriate people, and churchgoing had instilled in me that I was one of the people who deserved to be punished. Everything was destined to crumble and fall down around my shoulders, and it would be my fault. I always had prison in the back of my mind as a possibility, but it was lower on the list than stabbing myself with scissors or living in the street. My vision board would have been depressing, but accurate.

I felt that my life made the most sense as something locked away from the rest of humanity, quilted in a small room or barred away from others, it didn't matter which, only to be contained, to be reduced and small. The few times in my life that I tried to step out of that path, to try to get sober, to meet some new people, to allow myself to become interested in the woman who worked down the hall, I would be punished. I would be appropriately pressed down again, made to curl up in blankets, and watch that show where they sell samurai swords direct to camera. I made some honest efforts, but it always felt silly, like I was wearing someone else's clothes and realized ultimately that being a person was largely not to my liking, and I would get lost in my apartment and feel safe and slowly dissolve there.

I was like Walden, but if Walden was deeply afraid of the woods after a scarring childhood accident and a much worse person just in general.

I thought that my living on the first floor would satisfy or otherwise trick that drive to be contained, limit its impacts, delay my having to live outdoors. I was sandwiched between a neighbour and a dank basement, wrapped in blankets and often with my palms pressed against my ears to keep the sound of traffic out of my head.

It may have gone better with a downstairs neighbour, but I needed the basement. I tried to make it clear to whoever lived on the second floor that I technically also rent the basement. The basement was also my space, it was in the lease, and I slept on top of it like a dragon on jewels. Mine. You don't have access to the basement. I own it. You stay upstairs, never go down the basement where I keep boxes of my past and some private things. I needed some place private, secret. Leave me alone, for the love of god leave me alone.

It rarely worked. People don't pick up on nonverbal cues as much as they should, or maybe I was bad at it. Either way, people required more handholding than I was capable of and so I would yell at them. I left ten fucking signs all over the basement that said some version of "If you're reading this, you need to go back upstairs." It just made people want to know what's down there even more, and if I'd yelled at them, they'd want to do it out of spite, so they'd find excuses to sneak down there, and then they'd force me talk to them about what's down there. On and on until I'd become aggressive and loud, scaring them, eventually making their lives miserable until they'd move out of the building. My mother was right, noise really works, it drives people crazy. It drove me crazy.

Living downstairs meant that I'd hear their footsteps day and night, it also meant that I needed to deal with people all the time, every day, all day long. I had to hear them walking above me at all hours of the night, taking some sort of online dance class at 7 a.m. I lined my room with quilts, staple gunned five of them to the ceiling, it didn't matter, they came through all the same, it was like we lived in the same room. The floorboards didn't fit, they creaked and groaned, and all night long they just reminded you that you were never alone, no matter what you did, there were always people, people, people.

The most notable second floor neighbour, and the only good one, was a heavyset man in his late forties who woke up every morning and exercised for an hour. I can't imagine having the determination. It never made a difference, the last time I saw him he was as fat as the first. His footsteps were thunderous and he never lost an ounce. My favourite neighbour, simply because he never attempted to go into the basement, and picked up right away that I never, ever, under any circumstances, wanted to speak to him. Not even hello. I did the head nod and the pursed lip smile. If we were farther away, if we both pulled up to the house at the same time, and we were fifteen or more feet away, far enough that he might not spot the head nod and the pursed lips, I'd raise my hand in a wave that suggested my arm was on a string, being pulled up and away from me, turning me on my heel and away from the possibility of conversation.

I'd know him better eventually, unintentionally. Edgar. Edgar at first blush might be a murderer. He was the only person I've ever met that was more afraid of other people than I was. I loved Edgar. What a wonderful Edgar. We understood each other. Apart from his love of exercising, we might have been soulmates.

After Sunday breakfast I would be free of my father for another week, and I wouldn't start panicking about the next breakfast until late Wednesday or early Thursday. So, on Sunday afternoons, feeling full, feeling high above the surface of the waves, I would go grocery shopping. I'd buy a lot of vegetables because I would be hungover and I imagined every Sunday to be the last Sunday I would ever be hungover. It is time for Vegetable Alan. I would transform myself into a person who consumes only vegetables and gets in shape and finally gets it together enough to not quit a job moments before I am fired, and also, did you know, many recipes feature wine as an ingredient and that is why I am buying wine.

I will make a lovely pasta with vegetables and put a little red wine in the red sauce like Paul Prudhomme. When I get home, I will not drink the rest of the beer in the fridge, instead I will clean my house and open the windows and then around 6 p.m., after the apartment is clean, I will sauté the vegetables and begin cooking a perfectly delicious and healthy pasta, the smell of which will surely drive Edgar into a carbohydrate frenzy.

It's about noon when I leave the grocery store, the sun has baked the asphalt to its peak temperature, and I get sick next to my truck. It's September, there's a heatwave, it's 105°. Unseasonably warm. I squat behind the driver side door and breakfast leaves my body. When I'm done,

I climb into the driver's seat, recline it, and crank the air conditioning until I can see straight. I may have burst a blood vessel in my eye, my vision is blurred, I feel the pine needles under foot, and by the time my gait has been corrected, it's like my father was never there in the first place. No one can walk against the stream. There is only the path. There are always only the pine needles. I am always alone when there are pine needles.

The needles are in the exact same pattern. There are trees that I remember, things along the path that I remember. I remember the hawk circling towards the path, never touching it, and banking back towards the mountain. This is the beginning. Again. I will be on this path for weeks.

By the time I arrive at the twisted king tree in the clearing, the braided tree of trees, I am blank and numb and I barely notice that I've stopped. I am no longer walking. My body is mine again.

I am in the clearing in front of the tree.

Eek eek.

My mother was Catholic. A true believer. She didn't sit in the front pew every week, begging to be noticed by the Pastor like Greg Smith, she never even sat in the same seat. People got crazy about it at our church. She would come in just as the sermon was starting and sneak out the back the moment it was over. It was important to her, but it was only for her. There were no after-church functions, there were no prayer groups or gossip. She was there for the order and calm it brought to her life. She never said so exactly, I have no way of knowing if this was her plan. I was six, seven, eight. I was obsessed with the tiles on the floor.

The church was massive. A giant concrete building. Every wall was an unremarkable dark grey, brutal concrete. The few marks of colour were from Jesus' blood as he carried the cross through the twelve stations, each of which was marked by a Renaissance-style painting of Jesus' ornate suffering in a glittering gold frame. Jesus got the colour, Jesus gave the colour. Everywhere else was plain, sparse, and empty. Look at Jesus, behold the altar.

The altar was an explosion of colour. Red and gold, wealth and blood, donate or suffer. Large swaths of fabric hung from the ceiling and they would be rotated out with the seasons depending on the Christian calendar. Purple for lent, more red for Christmas, a sort of pale not-too-pink pink for Easter. Deep red carpet under a white and marble altar. Behind it, a remarkably lifelike Jesus, gruesome and horrifying to look at. I rarely could. I learned already, always look down. I'd lock into the tiles under the pew in front of me.

The tile beneath our feet was mosaic. Wedges of tile slivers, odd rectangles, and shapes. Nothing about it consistent, no pattern, just whatever they had left over, whatever was laying around. Pale yellow and light browns, almost identical in colour, the grout was some colour between the two. Maybe it was the same idea as casino carpet, make it boring, keep your eyes on the altar. A yellow with some brown flecks. Maybe it was boring from above three feet. But from my height, I could stare, lose focus, and pull the shapes together in my mind – seek out a series of triangles that made a dinosaur, a car, the ocean, a wave, a patch of pine trees. Just let my eyes blur a little bit so the chips and flakes of yellow tile blended into the rest, and there you were, standing in a clearing just below a twisted bunch of branches. No longer in church, but out in a clearing, lost in the tile you created. Maybe I am still there. Maybe I have lost my mind.

My mother did not like to feel like a burden. She shunned crowds apart from church and rarely left the house except to work. My father was essentially the same. So when I was young I mostly skipped the process of making friends, I didn't know that it was something important. People were for other people.

My mother didn't believe in heaven and hell because they seemed like the same place. "It all sounds the same." She mostly focused on the parts of the sermons that dealt with the afterlife. She wanted to know how it all worked. She wanted to know the rules.

"Just keep coming to church and you'll get to where you're supposed to go."

"But how do you know that? What if I'm different?"

Her chats with the pastor were difficult. He felt challenged, that she was questioning his knowledge, or worse, her faith. But she just wanted a checklist. She believed. She just wanted to arrange the tiles on the floor. "I got it. Heaven. Hell. Purgatory. I understand. How will I know when I am done? How will I know when enough is enough?"

The week before she disappeared, we went to church and I let my eyes lose focus to see if I could find the knight I'd built the week before, but before I had time to really look, she'd grabbed me by the bicep and was dragging me out the door. "What horseshit," she said. "What utter horseshit." I don't remember what the sermon was about. I remember the knight had a crooked lance with an arrow tip. Like a lightning bolt.

She stopped the car in front of the house, reached

across me to open the door for me, ushered me out of the car, and then she was gone. She didn't even look over. She didn't seem disturbed about anything one way or the other. It was like she was going to the store. But a few days later, my father was shaking me by the shoulders. Wake up, he said. Wake up, we found her.

My father and I met for breakfast on Sunday. We were both hungover. He talked about the Phillies, about the weather. I felt the space between my lips and my teeth with the tip of my tongue. Dry. Like sandpaper. I must have been smoking again. I learned an interesting thing about smoking. I smoked about a pack-and-a-half a week but only when I was drunk, when I was sober I had no use for cigarettes. I never felt addicted. I never needed a smoke. I needed to drink. When I was drunk, I needed cigarettes to live. Drunk Alan was addicted to cigarettes. Sober Alan found them disgusting. It's like I was two different people with two entirely different chemistries, walking along the same meandering path to nowhere. Somewhere between Two-Beer Alan and Five-Beer Alan, Cigarette Alan springs to life.

I smoked cigarettes three to five days a week. It was enjoyable, all of the advertising was right. One of the greatest joys in my life is that I have no idea if Edgar cared if I smoked. I smoked extra for Edgar. I liked to indulge in his silence after so many lousy neighbours who would complain that it was coming through their vents or that I had crashed my car into the bushes. Edgar.

Now is a good time to talk about Edgar. Edgar was one of the few people in my life that I truly cared for, who I think truly cared for me. We eventually got to know each other, by accident, when a tree fell through the roof of the duplex. It took an act of god to get me to talk to someone, and it was just to see if they were dead. When it turned out he wasn't, that he was alive, that the branch had pierced through the top of his house and clear through his kitchen, but he was in the other room pointlessly exercising, saving his life in a different way than would be expected, I was disappointed. Because it meant that I would be deeply uncomfortable talking to another person, instead of just being mildly uncomfortable at the sight of a dead body. Third worst would have been having to intervene in some way, to have to bravely lift a tree off of Edgar's pinned and stubborn body.

But he was fine, he let me in to survey the damage and in that moment I realized he thought I was the landlord, which I regret not exploiting in any way. His apartment was nicer than mine, there were things that had previously been on shelves scattered across the floor from the impact of the tree. Little trinkets, hummels, things that had been collected on his various travels. He took the moment to walk me around the apartment, pointing into the various rooms, and naming them. "This is the bathroom, this is the bedroom, this is the living room," as though our apartments were not in the same building, directly stacked on top of each other, in the same exact layout. He was a nice man. I walked three steps behind him as the cold air whipped in through the hole in the ceiling, a reality television show was on way too low, with the subtitles on. "I'm always worried it's on too loud, so I turn it way down and put the subtitles on." Edgar.

The landlord gave us a common enemy, which is the only way I ever learned to make friends. I corner a third party and isolate them into evil. It is what I learned from my family, it is how my father and I still operated, it is why we tipped one waitress really high, and the rest really low. On average, we got to tip less than we would if we tipped everyone equally, and we got free things from the one waitress and impeccable service from the others. It always pays to be creatively cruel to those around you.

Everyone hates their landlord, it is a natural part of life. It is the hierarchy. Edgar's roof took entirely too long to get fixed. I don't know how long it is supposed to have taken, but was easier to stay friendly with Edgar if I helped him feel miserable about the situation. It worked, and we commiserated. I found myself lingering in the car, trying to time my entrance into the building so that it would match his arrival home from work. He worked in accounting. He was meticulous and quiet and in accounting. He worked on spreadsheets all day, and I told him I liked things just so also. I did not tell him that I ruined everything in spite of myself and never kept anything just so — that way I'd always be disappointed in my surroundings and use it as an excuse to drink.

My social life having not had any oxygen for almost twenty years exploded endorphins through my brain and directly into poor Edgar's face. It was the same rush of emotion I got when my father agreed with me, when he looked at me in the eyes, it was a nearly new sensation and it was overwhelming and I didn't really enjoy it, but I felt it like a need and it got to be that he was all I could think about. I was not in love with Edgar, I don't think, but I didn't really like Edgar either — he was boring and he didn't drink until I started hinting that he should — I just had fit Edgar into my routine. It was very exciting to have someone to ask "How about this weather?" I always heard people asking other people dumb shit like that and I never understood it, and then there was Edgar. Me and Edgar and the weather against the landlord, and by proxy, the world.

Edgar needed to be out of his house for long stretches of time. He worked like a normal person, so it was rarely an issue, but occasionally the crew fixing his roof or the water damage would need to work nights and I wasn't doing anything, so the two of us got in the habit of taking walks. Just the two of us, neighbours, out for neighbourly walks. It wasn't long before I got bored of the walks, of fighting my way through conversation, and coaxed him into a bar so we could drink instead. He wasn't much of a drinker, but I did my part for the both of us.

On our last visit to the bar I told him that my mother had a secret friend too, someone she cared about too much to mention, someone who she'd explore the neighbourhood with. A beautiful woman I met only once, in the receiving line at her funeral, who hugged me like we were family and disappeared the next day. "Colorado." I said. "My mom died but she got to go to Colorado."

Edgar left the bar before I did, I don't remember when. I don't remember when I left either. This would be the last time we speak. Poor Edgar. What a shame to have met me.

Eek Eek.

I am in the clearing in front of the King tree and there is something behind me, walking loudly, metallically, shoving trees out of the way. Breaking branches. It is horrifying, but it is different. I have not heard these sounds in ages. I remember metal. I remember these sounds. I assume it is coming for me, maybe to kill me, but that's okay. I am not walking, and that is all that matters.

I am motion sick from stillness. I still feel as though I am moving, walking, phantom limbs move forward, wobble me back and forth, even in this blessed stillness

I feel as though I am being conveyed, forward, into the tree, then suddenly I am. I walk forwards into the clearing, turn right, and sit down on a fallen log. I watch the trees sway with the force of whatever metal is moving through them, mostly I am overjoyed to be seated.

My father and I were at breakfast again and he started talking about the Iran–Contra. I still don't know what that is, and I don't think he ever knew either. He just kept saying that something was like the Iran–Contra. And I finally said, "I don't know what you're talking about." And it was like he was waiting for me to say that so that he could say, "Well, of course you don't." Then he threw his arms up and gestured at me with both hands. *What an idiot I am saddled with, can you believe this idiot, Perfect Pancakes? I am sorry you had to hear this, Perfect Pancakes.*

It was not the first time I had walked out on breakfast, but it was the last. I hurried back to my truck, but still heard him yell "Where are you going? Prima donna!" over the heat. 106°. October 1st. It's just unseasonably warm.

"Work!" I shouted back, lying. There was no more work, the last of my jobs was done for a while. It'd be years until I worked again.

After you've been through a few jobs falling apart, you start to see the signs. Not talking to anyone is fine at the beginning of any job — you get away with it because you are so focused on learning. Your learning supersedes talking to the other office employees. After a while, when it becomes clear that you are not interested in being friends with the rest of the telemarketing department, your work becomes more suspect — ordinary mistakes or woozily responding to questions through the deep throb of your headache all become magnified and transparent. What was regarded briefly as deep concentration, was in fact, trying not to get sick in the middle of a too-warm conference room.

It feels to them that you are always late or always something else. It's impossible not to be nervous about it and I just go deeper into myself. I make it worse by talking even less. I make other people nervous. Two jobs ago, I was keeping it together pretty well, not drinking until after work, keeping regular hours, sleeping well, and eating right for once. Then I heard someone ask, out loud, like I wasn't sitting right there, to nobody in particular: "Who's the nervous guy?" I didn't turn around even though I knew he meant me, because if I turned around and he did mean me, I'd always be "Nervous Guy." At the water cooler, in the parking structure. Day after day, "What's up nervous guy?"

"That's just Alan. He's behind on some things." I was not, but the hook had been set. I was now everyone's reason why. Why did this account leave? "I don't know, maybe ask Alan?" Quiet and meek don't go far in an office environment. Psychos advance. People who do not care about other people. I don't care about other people. I care about other people caring about me, which is a subtle but deeply important difference. People who don't care about other people caring about them — those are the people who climb the ladder, you get a lot accomplished when you don't have to hurdle your failures every morning. They climb the ladder and then saw the ladder out from under them so you can't climb up, then throw coconuts at your head. These are the people who breeze around the mountain unscathed, these are not the people who crumble to rubble, who can't take the eyes on them, who don't mind the endless tasks, who cannot be harmed.

Untouchable, flawless, fire or no fire, they are going to be the first person to the top, even if the prize at the summit is worthless. Or heaven. Or whatever. They would not be mesmerized by pine needles or tile floor, would not seek outside of themselves for answers. They would not be sitting on a tree trunk, looking at a knight they created in their mind when they were eight. They would not be so obviously dead, and so unable to accept it.

3.

"Alan."

"Hi."

"Alan." The knight is forty feet tall. His sword is exactly as I remember, bigger than him, cobbled together from tiny yellow tiles. He is fuzzy at the edges; he is difficult to find as he moves against the pale bark of the twisted tree. The sword drags behind him, its arrowhead tip trenching the ground as he walks. He is moving slowly and with purpose, but the sword drags and he is holding his side.

"Alan, help me." He falls towards me and shatters into a million yellow shards at my feet and I scream until my eyes blur and I am walking alone in the forest.

Eek eek. Eek eek.

I am permitted to pass the clearing this time. The shards of the knight still blurry and visible in my periphery as I pass, locked into my steady motion. I am not allowed to rest on the tree stump, or walk freely in the clearing. I am back in the motions. I have learned not to fight it. I am letting go.

When I make it to the blue hallway, I have a more obedient companion. He does not try to run, he does not go mad at the endlessness of the blue. We walk, perfect partners. Somewhere ahead I know the beach is coming. We will land on the beach and be separated forever. My vision blurs and I wish him well, and I am on my knees in the sand. To my right, a woman falls and slices her hand on a shell, her blood drip drops and we all follow behind. I take my place somewhere in the middle of the line.

I am being shaken awake. I am being pressed forcefully into the earth. There is a light in my eyes and sand in my mouth. "Let's go, buddy. Get up." My teeth chattered, all by themselves. I regained consciousness as I was being ushered towards a police car. I didn't remember what was going on, so I asked "What's going on?" No response, I was urged forward, with my arms behind me, my gait uneven and stilted. "What's going *onnnnn*?"

About twenty minutes later, I get booked for being drunk in public. Ocean City, New Jersey is a dry town. You're allowed to bring your own alcohol across the border, you can drink it, but you cannot buy it within city limits and you cannot drink it on public property. In Ocean City, drinking is to be done in the home. Or, say, on a fourth floor balcony. The police officers didn't get this reference, and only repeat that my alcohol was with me, on the beach, where I would have frozen to death had they not found me. They wasted time telling me to feel lucky, alcohol thins the blood, they say, and we don't run so many patrols in the off season.

Late summers in those days didn't last as long, and shifted into fierce winters, bypassing fall altogether. When the officers finish their sermon, I am left alone in a small cell. No bars, just a big door I can't open, next to a long metal bench. I was comfortable freezing to death on the beach, and somehow the metal bench felt colder. Passing time in a drunk tank is horrible. There's nothing to focus on but the growing sensation of reality creeping back into your body as you sober up. I sat on a cold metal bench until I felt the shame of it kick in. The only escape was sleep. I pressed my face into the cold metal and, mercifully, I drifted away again.

This has happened before.

The last time I'd woken up in jail, it was different. Worse. Less embarrassing but more terrifying. I didn't remember being collected. I remembered being at the bar. I was there, alone, drinking. I was talking to a man and his friend, wedging my way into their conversation. It was early, I was more drunk than the clock suggested I should be. They didn't want to talk to me. I kept it up, and they moved. I moved with them. We shouted at each other and suddenly I woke up in a room with a door I could not open and I panicked and screamed and pounded the door with my fists. "Let me out, what's going on?" Still too drunk to make sense of the context clues.

They let me scream for hours. Eventually someone came by and explained. "You are in a holding cell. You were found vomiting on the corner of Grand and McCallister. When a police officer tried to help you, you resisted and he nearly tased you. Instead you got in the back of a squad car and were placed here. In a holding cell. You will be released in the morning. Stop screaming." But I didn't. And the pieces of the night fell together in my head one after the other. Being in the car, explaining myself. "I live nearby. I'm walking home. I'm not driving. I'm not driving. I'm walking home. I live nearby." I remember walking through the parking structure. Passing other police officers. Hearing them laugh. I remember picking my father up from the drunk tank when I was eighteen. Little bits of memory fragments drifted through my pounding head and I calmed down and slept it off and swore I'd never drink again.

The day I was released from the Ocean City Precinct I wandered Ocean City, looking for my car, finally deciding to get a motel room until the hangover calmed down. I would begin again tomorrow. I can't keep doing this, I told myself. I have had my last drink.

Of course, I parked the car across the street from where they found my mother. I wandered to everywhere else I could think of. I don't remember driving sixty-five miles. The whole experience erased from memory. I have to start over. This has to end. At some point this has to end.

I had to borrow money from my father to pay the fine. I knew he didn't have it either. But he's my father, I reasoned. He had to take care of me. Those are the rules. He was always my father. I was always his son. He always had to take care of me. If he didn't want to pay Ocean City public drunkenness fines, he shouldn't have had a child.

He shouldn't have married my weird mother. She should have kept me safe from my weird father. They both should have kept me from becoming this mess.

The woman is being pressed into the pavement, the sea of us has parted for each of us to witness it and in the instant after I pass, I am walking in the forest. I am alone in the pines.

When I was fifteen I had to collect my father once a week from different bars and alleys he'd pass out or be knocked out in. I was a teenager. He was drunk and largely unemployed. We were using each other and my mother to do whatever we wanted. He was drinking. I was also drinking. But I was a teenager, it was part of what we did. He was in his thirties and it was depressing. My involvement in his drinking was embarrassing, infuriating. He started losing teeth. He was working nights as security at the mall where my classmates all hung out and sometimes we'd see him as we left the movies, arriving for his shift disheveled in his car, asleep, half dressed in his uniform that he was still paying off. The mall made him buy a badge. They loaned him money so he could buy a badge from them. So that he could walk back and forth in a closed mall, for eight hours with a break for lunch at 3 a.m. He figured out where the cameras were in the first week, and took sips from a flask that he'd refill at lunch. He'd come home drunker than when he went in. He was fired long before he was able to fully pay back the badge and uniform. He kept it anyway and I made sure he was buried with it in his top breast pocket. I told everyone it was important to him.

He worked there exactly long enough for my friends to find out that the security guard with the missing teeth was my father.

Fourteen through eighteen. Those were my prime years for friendship development. Those were the years I really gave it a shot, really tried to be a normal person who enjoyed being around people, and tried to feel that people enjoyed being around me. I tried. Four years of trying and failing. Of being the weirdo that everyone walked the long way around. It just didn't take. Wasn't for me. You do things when you are young that you lose in adulthood. Nobody plays dodgeball past a certain point, except assholes. I was like that but with other human beings.

By the time I was seventeen, I'd largely abandoned the concept and settled into myself as a person who spent most of his time with movies and alcohol. It was an easier path to take. The internet helped a lot. It had a lot of the same appeal as drinking. You just sort of fade into it: you check Facebook, then you check your email, then you check something else, then you check something else, and you just keep clicking on whatever is next and before you know it, it's time to sleep, and you didn't have to leave your house or talk to anyone and another day has been spent disappearing even more completely.

When I see my father again, walking impossibly against the flow of people, his wounds are more pronounced but he's still smiling. We're all still walking in our path, but he's aged, he's older than he was when he died. His wounds have spread, they seem filthy, he is not walking as confidently. When he appears in the distance, I know that it is him, I have seen him hundreds of times now. But always the same. Always the same smile. The same gait. He is feeble and pathetic and the hate rises in me with such strength it surprises me and I anticipate my vision blurring. I wait for the beautiful smell of pine. I allow myself to hate him fully just to throw myself deep into the loneliness of the pines.

We were inert for years. From the age of nine to fourteen, it was mostly just television and waiting. He would urge me to bed earlier and earlier as the week progressed. In the early years he did not like to drink in front of me, but that passed as his humanity faded and his tethers to fatherhood slipped through his fingers. When he was on his good run, in the months after she died, he was better. More fulfilled as a person, making more money. But he was exhausted. There was less chaos, less uncertainty, but more distance. It had its pros and cons. I had cereal, new clothes, but still no father. Later there was no cereal but too much father. It was bad in either direction. The one time I spoke to a therapist, the one time I really gave it a shot, I told him this. And he suggested I was in mourning for my lost childhood. That I needed to fully let it go in order to move forward. But I didn't know which one to let go of. Which version would I be left with? Wouldn't choosing one path or the other leave me with nothing? I'd just repeat the process. I'd have to rebuild from scratch.

He said that was mostly the point of therapy and I cut our session short and never saw him again. It cost $95 and was almost certainly a scam. I thought about keying his car. He had a personalized plate with a doctor pun on it. I didn't key it. I just went home. It was close enough to walk and I took my time. I tried to be anything but angry and it didn't work, so I kicked over people's trash cans as I went. Every third trash can. I don't know why.

This was also the night I found Jesse Smith on Facebook and looked at his family until I couldn't take it anymore and wound up in the bathroom with a pair of scissors.

My father and I met for breakfast on Sunday. This would be the final time. My father had lost another tooth. He was looking older than usual these days. Even with the shitty moustache that he thought covered up the lack of teeth and the yellow that was starting to cloud the corners of his eyes. His liver is clearly failing, I thought. And for some reason, I figured, today's the day. Let's get into it.

"Why do you think she did it?" I'd never asked him. I never cared what he thought. He'd made plenty of jokes about it, trying to deflect from whatever it was that he thought I thought about it. But I never really heard him talk. And if the yellow kept pooling in his eyes and I didn't ask, I'd never know. But he didn't say anything. He talked for a half an hour about how they never should have gotten together in the first place. How it was something that he thought was going to be quick and over and done with but she was religious, she had a family, she had a church, they had to be official and good and clean and above all, normal, and all he ever wanted to do was nothing. Same as me. So he worked every angle he could to do as little as possible, and probably in the process doing twice as much as everyone else. "Working is the most important thing a man can do." It was just in his brain. His brain was full of these catchphrases that he supposedly lived his life by, a code of gallantry from afternoon television in his empty house.

His parents were gone, had never bothered with him, another set of eastern Pennsylvania drunks. His father worked in a warehouse, his mother worked wherever she could. It was a folk song come to life but with all the extra additional actual sadness baked in. They were all miserable. They lived in a grey house that eventually fell over, fell into the dirt, and was absorbed back into the earth, he thought. "Maybe they bulldozed it but who the fuck knows. It's gone. There's a pathmark there now, little shitty mini mall." He left as soon as he could and never went back, never heard from them again. Found out they died via a postcard from his uncle. Carbon monoxide poisoning. They both went in their sleep. They were living in Upstate New York of all places. Funny thing to have happen, to be there one minute and gone the next.

We ate eggs and bacon and coffee and talked about his past, about his wife, about his son, and none of it meant anything at all so we went drinking.

I am standing in the clearing again, but it is quiet. There is no clanking behind me. The knight has been swept up, my eyes are guided upwards and I am allowed a moment of calm, watching the branches wave, until there is a glint in the clouds. I watch as his sword falls out of the sky and splits the twisted tree like lightning. It erupts into flames right down the centre. My arms belong to me and I am able to hold them up to shield my eyes from the light. My hands are wrinkled, the skin folding over thick knobby knuckles. Aged. Like I'd lived to be a thousand. I try to move them but I can't, not for any invisible resistance, they just ache. I just ache.

The tree burns in front of me and I am forced to watch it burn to ash until my vision blurs and I am walking in the tall grass and the crickets say eek eek.

My father and I go drinking at the bar by his house. He was a regular, and everyone there knew him and knew to keep away from him. He had his own section of the bar by the video poker machine that had a little sign saying "for entertainment purposes only," but the bar paid out all the same. When we arrived, for lack of other things to talk about, he focused on the poker machine. We both have something to focus on instead of each other, so he tried to teach me how to play. He told me which bets were for suckers, and which were for real players like us, people who knew this machine inside out and backwards. He told me about how he wouldn't let people near the machine unless they listened to his warnings and tips first. If they didn't listen, they didn't get to play. I listened.

The machine impassively took dollar after dollar from him. The credit counter in the started at $20 and screen slowly drained out, incrementing occasionally when he hit jacks or better. There was never any doubt that the whole $20 was going to disappear, but he is surprised when it does, furious. He pounded the bar with his left fist. The linoleum was worn where he pounded. He had made this mark thousands of times, over and over, almost worn a hole through it.

Once his money was gone, he let me have a turn. His teachings were complete. I fed a $20 into the machine and he looked over my shoulder, telling me what buttons to press, but not why, and we watch together as my $20 takes the same slightly bumpy path to zero as his did. He started pressing the buttons himself when the end was in sight, when the $20 had been replaced by an "8" made of two stacked squares on the screen. He slapped the back of his hand against the eight, and said that I must have done something wrong, that I didn't have the timing right. "You don't have the touch. It's a problem for a lot of people. Not everybody gets the touch." He elbowed me out of the way and asked for another $20 before the first one was gone. It is 11 a.m. We'd burn through $300 before we left, but I don't remember much of it. He spent most of the last hour of his life mashing buttons, taking $20 after $20 from my stack.

I understood what we were doing. I knew the direction we were headed. We hadn't drank together in many years, but it felt familiar, I could see the horizon approaching and it felt like I was seventeen again. The two of us loading up, and in a while, we will explode. For a while, I was in control, watching him mash buttons, but mostly I was trying to keep up, to prove to him that we were equals, and even though the thought of that was about the worst thing I could think of, it would have been nice to be like someone else. To have not felt quite so alien.

I had a Budweiser with him to start, but once he is lost in the machine and I am sitting quietly to his side, I switch to whisky. I knew where we were going, and I wanted to get there as quickly as possible.

As I remember it, I was doing okay until he hit me in the ribs with a pool cue. He didn't have the coordination, and the bar is not wide enough to deserve a pool table, so most of his power went into the wall he clipped before the cue bounced into my side. It wasn't enough to do any permanent damage, but I still went down and sucked air. He would have kicked me in the face, but the bartender was on him quickly enough to stop it.

It doesn't matter. We made amends on the curb, in the afternoon heat. I told him I'd drive him home. It was only around the corner, but it was so damn hot.

I was so happy when he died. I didn't have any other

reaction. I was mostly just thrilled to be rid of him. There were complications and there was court and all the rest of it, but goddamn I was so happy he was dead.

In the moment I didn't have a lot to go on, I'd never killed anybody before. But it felt okay. I always thought I should feel bad about it, but I never did. He killed my mother. I killed him. Someone else will kill me. Probably me, I figured. When I kill me I'll pin that on him too. So really, we'll have killed each other. I thought that someday, I would work up the guts to find a rafter and a rope and pin a note to my chest that just says his name, or something like that. I never figured out the details and it turned out not to matter anyway.

After he died, I thought I should go to church and ask for absolution, or just to talk to someone and find out, maybe finally find out if I'm going to heaven or hell, if my mother went to heaven or hell, if my father will ever get out of hell. Could a person get out of hell? If they did, could they come find me if I am not in hell? If we are both in hell, do we have to see each other? Would that be part of the punishment? Would I be made to see him at the cafeteria in hell, or at town hall meetings? Would we need to be together at all, or could we finally be apart? Could I finally be alone and free of them both? But I never sought anyone out, I didn't talk to anyone. My mother did all that work and she came to some certain conclusion. I don't know what the details of that conclusion were but it certainly made an impression on her.

I had one good weekend in my childhood. My father wasn't there. My mother decided she needed a weekend away, and we went where everybody went, where everybody goes, where everyone will always go. We went to the Jersey Shore. She rented the house we always rented, the one she'd jump from, and we just went and she said we could do whatever I wanted. I tried every ride. I went to every arcade. I think this was probably a test. I had so much pizza. I think she thought this would be the last weekend together. I had so much ice cream. I think she was going to do it this weekend, I think she was going to have one good weekend with me and then cut loose, but something happened this weekend to make her stick around and I'll never know what it was. I got four hundred tickets from the skee ball machine and maybe I said something to her that made her stay, and then I said something else later that made her leave. I think about that weekend every three days, on average, for the rest of my life.

My father's good stretch at work, the stability stretch, seemed to be harder on him as it went along. During the initial phase, it felt like he was getting over on the system. They all really felt bad for him because he'd lost his wife. He would come home, and talk to me, his only friend, his nine-year-old son who would never recover: "They just let me do whatever I want, and whatever I want is just great. 'It's okay, you take your time.' Everyone just gets out of my way. Nobody wants to look at me. Nobody looks at anything I'm doing or anything I'm planning on doing. I left in the middle of the day for four hours. Nobody said boo. Boo hoo. Booooooo hooooo."

I got pulled out of class for attacking a boy who made a joke about my mom. We were in gym class, and he said one of those 'Your mom's so fat' jokes, and I threw a basketball into his face and bloodied his nose. I had to be pulled off of him. It would happen three more times in the next three years. I calmed down around fourteen. But prior to that, I would attack classmates if I didn't feel like doing any more work. It was a get out of class free card. I wasn't a bully. I went after the bigger kids. I would just lunge for their stomach so if they fought back, they wouldn't have the leverage to do much damage. I'd go home and watch cartoons. I'd get to be a little boy unaccompanied in the world on a school day. It was wonderful. The only true freedom I have ever felt in my life was walking the streets as a ten-year-old on a Tuesday afternoon.

My dad never found out as far as I know. The school had our phone number but I think we'd been written off a few years before my mother even died. We were adrift. Something that would clunk into the side of town every few months, cause a problem, and drift away again. It would have made sense to be the kind of family who moved around a lot. It would have made sense for my father to be a migrant farmer, drifting from town to town. Grifters. When I felt like I should have had a better relationship with my father, I imagined us as grifters. Selling magic tonics from the back of a truck, or pulling scams together. We were too lazy for all that, but we were equals, always on the same footing from the age of nine onwards. We both added the same amount of value to each other's lives and we were largely a drain on the rest of society. We were stationary and wilting. Waiting for our lives to run their respective, identical courses.

What follows is my routine. My arc. The loop that I was never able to escape, never really intended to escape, the path that I walked my entire life, wearing the tread deeper and deeper with each pass, making it nearly impossible to escape even if I wanted to:

I wake up hungover, exhausted, with a crushing dread in my chest that I cannot explain. It's noon or later. I am drenched in sweat and my head pounds so profoundly that I think about killing myself to get it to stop. I curl tightly into a ball and breathe as deeply as possible. I will sometimes fall back asleep, sometimes I will think about the past and cry. An hour later or so I will call a pizza shop and order more food than any person should eat in three days.

I make a full pot of coffee. I drink the coffee before the pizza arrives. It increases my already frantic heart rate to an impossible pace. It skips every so often and every time it does, I think that I am dying. I brace myself for the impact and there is something not quite like relief when it passes.

I eat the food, I eat all of it, even if I am sick from drinking, there is nothing that will cure a hangover like grease, supposedly. I have not experienced any evidence that this is true, I have only ever experienced the opposite. I drink Gatorade if the pizza place has Gatorade. If not, I put three tablespoons of sugar in tap water and mix it up. I fill my stomach so completely that it is difficult to move and I am forced by the limits of my insides to go back to bed or the couch. If I have a couch at the time of this experience.

I watch movies about the Old West or YouTube videos about distant and secluded places. I watch videos about beautiful twenty-somethings who live in tiny spaces, or in the sides of hills, or in the backs of vans. I watch them for tips and tricks on how to be a better poor person. I look for branding techniques that I could apply to my own YouTube channel or blog if I was ever to start something like that. I watch in awe and I promise myself that I will start something like that. All I have to do is quit drinking and get in better shape. I will quit drinking and get in better shape and live in a ridiculous scenario so that other people can look at me doing that. I do not like people but would really enjoy a steady drip of approval that a view counter would provide. I think about ways to build a shed out of pallet wood and do not think about the fact that I do not own a hammer and wonder vaguely if the pallet wood would off-gas and give me cancer. I begin to dismiss the idea of being creatively poor and attractive. It starts to feel ridiculous that I even thought of it in the first place. I can't even get to a place where I can live in a way that is not depressing. I think about this as I drift off to sleep, or I get up and make the attempt to clean up my apartment but am limited by my headache and so I just lay back down and watch pornography until I fall asleep again.

When I wake up I get back to drinking. Evan Williams. I drink one handle of it each day when I am on my game. It is a complete mind eraser. I am gone. Floating by noon. I usually run out for more around 5 p.m. I drive. I have never been pulled over. It is not very far and I am a very good driver. I get two more bottles. When I get home, the emotions kick in around 6 p.m. and I either play music loud enough for Edgar to hear and I dance or weep.

If it is Sunday, I am filled with dread that the following day is Monday. I repeat the previous day. If there are holes in my walls from the emotional surge, I think about fixing them, or having the cuts on my knuckles looked at, and decide to do neither.

If it is Monday, I wake up filled with dread that it is Monday. I arrive to work late, if at all, and I am mostly frozen by my fear of the experience and of other people. Of doing everything wrong. I am still hungover from Saturday, if not Sunday. I do not talk to anyone; if I do, it is awkward and I say the wrong thing. Something grotesque or evil. I worry about saying things that I would never say, of being so completely consumed by anxiety that I just say the wrong thing just to have said the wrong thing, to get it over with so I can get to the part where I really shine: Apologizing. There is nothing in this world I am better at than apologizing. You should see me on a crowded bus. I am a pinball of apology, I am in the way more than anyone else is in the way: Sorry. I'm sorry. I'm so sorry.

After work I come home and am so thoroughly exhausted from existing in the world with people that I just order food. I order delivery, I don't talk to the driver, I apologize for some reason as I tip. I over tip. I do not have any money. I am waiting to be fired.

I am fired. I get fired for showing up late/not at all, for drinking before and after work, but mostly for being such a sparkler of anxiety that I am difficult to be around. I am sorry. I say, without meaning to, at every job I start that "I can't believe I got this job." As a rule, nobody wants to hear that you are flabbergasted by your own ability to acquire a job they are paying you to do. This is generally the first gentle push of the first domino. And a few weeks later, I am correct. I am fired. The relief of it is staggering. Being fired, being told that under no circumstances am I to appear in this building with these people ever again, is like a cool breeze on a hot day. Dear god, thank you so much.

I allow myself to be depressed by the firing but also for being the person that I am who is thrilled to be fired, for being completely unable to hold down a job and being so delighted by all of it that I spend my last pay cheque on alcohol because the only thing more frightening than not having any money is not having any alcohol.

I wake up hungover and exhausted with a crushing

dread in my chest that I cannot explain. It's noon or later. I half-heartedly send resumes into the ether while I watch YouTube videos of better lives and let that be good enough.

After a few weeks, I run almost completely out of money and I call my father for help. He never has any money either. But it is his job to help me. I am his son. These are the rules.

This is how it happened: My father and I were driving home from a bar, I don't remember which. I was driving, he was in the passenger seat screaming at me about something. I do not know what. I wasn't able to respond, it hurt to breath, even through the alcohol. He'd hit me with a pool cue earlier that afternoon. Somehow it's 8 p.m. This day would be the most time we'd spent together in twenty years. I remember thinking that, even for me, I was pretty drunk, maybe the drunkest I'd ever been. I don't remember much of the night, and I later will swear to police officers that I don't remember this part either, and say only that he attacked me again and grabbed the wheel. He screams and no matter how much I scream back, he doesn't stop screaming. He tells me my life has been a failure, how it is somehow, miraculously, more of a failure than his own. That I have used my mother's death as an excuse my whole life. He says that if I hadn't been born she would still be alive. He begins to say something else, but I put my foot down as far as it will go, and drive us into a cement lane divider. I am wearing a seatbelt and he is not, it is a late '90s Tercel, made before passenger side airbags, and the better part of his torso leaves the car and he dies on the hood of my car before I regain consciousness.

The sirens woke me. While I waited for them to arrive, I left my head on the steering wheel and watched as the steam from the radiator bloomed around his body and it carried him into the night.

I am allowed to continue through the grasshopper field without assistance. I could use the assistance. I am in my seventies, probably. Maybe eighties. I am struggling. The grasshoppers are the same as they always have been. It occurs to me now, that I should have named them. They are familiar, old friends. I can spot the differences between them. Different jump heights. Different wingspans. Subtle note changes in the eeks. "Eek eek," I say, "eeek eek." I try to match them one to one. I eek eek with their eek eeks and I can smell the dirt beneath my feet and eek eek I say. Eek eek.

My mother's loop was tighter. More controlled. She was a regimented person and thought that if she did things in a certain way, certain other things would happen. If she kept the house clean, the marriage would make sense or stay out of her mind altogether. If she had a child, she would like children, be like everyone else. If she worked hard and saved, her husband would appreciate the fact that he had to do so little, instead of wallowing in it so completely. There were rules. Good people went to heaven. Bad people went to hell. Everyone else went to purgatory.

Every day she woke up before I did. She made the three of us lunches. She may have snuck cigarettes. My father swore she smoked but he could never catch her in the act. He swore that cigarettes were missing and that he was pretty sure that I wasn't taking them. It is likely that he forgot how many he smoked or was unable to open a box, a door, move from room to room without seeing conspiracies, without spotting reasons for his own shortcomings. Most of what I know comes to me through him.

I was nine. She dropped me at school at 7:15. Most kids didn't arrive until 8. I was there forty-five minutes early and only forty-five minutes after I woke up. My father said it was as much of me as she could handle. I walked home.

She worked late. She liked to work. There were rules. My father talked about her as if she was full of gears, a wind-up thing that had come to life. "Everything had to be just fuckin so."

She came home and made everything just fuckin so. We mostly ordered in. She didn't cook, neither did my father, neither do I. When we sat at the table, everything would bounce up and down from the pumping of her left leg. A piston. Up and down, up and down forever. It wasn't something you'd notice after a while, but your drink always had ripples in it. She ate quickly, meticulously, and didn't seem to enjoy it. Never made a sound. It was power for the piston. That was all. She had to get out. Out out out.

She took a walk after dinner. She said it was something they did as a family when she was young, but she was inconsistent with the details. Sometimes she said they all walked as a family, but if I asked if I could come along, she would shift, say that her mother walked alone, and it was something that she liked to do alone also. It was "for the lord." She would walk for two, sometimes three, hours. My dad thought she was out there smoking his cigarettes. He would say so, or he would silently check his pack and count. He was unable to count without moving his mouth. I stared at the television set and tried not to make any noise so he didn't slap me with his hat and shout at me to shut up and focus.

She came in the back door, having left from the front, she would appear from the basement and it was entirely possible that she walked out the front door, walked immediately around the house, and snuck in the basement. She would appear dry when it was raining, warm when it was cold.

I saw her for less than an hour a day. I begged for her attention and was slapped with his hat, or a pillow, or spritzed with condensation from his drink when I did so. I sat still. I tried to focus.

Somewhere in this mix I assume she thought often and lovingly about death and how great it would be to be dead. It scared her probably, and she would go upstairs, leaving us to the television, and she would read novels and the bible.

She'd call down to me at 8 p.m. and I would be so ready for it that I'd stare at the top of the staircase from 7:45, checking the top of the staircase like it was a pack of cigarettes.

"Alan. Bedtime." I would explode up the stairs. I'd only ever occasionally catch the side of her as she closed her bedroom door.

As near as I can tell, my father's loop was nearly identical to mine. He drank beer and barely ate, but other than that, I followed his footsteps and he followed mine. We walked in circles together, carrying each other along to nowhere, wearing a hole in the floor to fall into, to die in.

The blue hallway has been remodeled. It has been painted green. It extends on forever and I am granted company. I am locked in motion, under control. I cannot turn my head. I can smell her all the same, and I walk the green hallway with my mother. Her wrists have healed. They are brand new.

My son was born on a Thursday afternoon. Almost nine months to the day after I'd been released from prison.

I did five beautiful years. No drinking. No speaking. I learned to meditate. I thought often about my father and how happy I was to have killed him. I felt thankful to alcohol for giving me the strength and guiding me to this fate. I surrendered myself to its power and it paid back in spades.

Every day in prison, with my clear head, and my healthy body, I stretched, I read books. I spoke to no one. I was a monk. It was the best five years of my life. People make a lot of fuss about prison, that it's dangerous, violent. That you're in a place with terrible people and they'll all kill you or rape you the second you're not looking. That was not my experience. Violence happened when people spoke. When people didn't apologize. When people got stir crazy and missed the outside. I never spoke but to apologize and would have stayed forever if they let me.

I knew from the second I entered prison that I would resume drinking the second I walked out. I was sentenced to ten years, but I was released in five for being a quiet nobody. I don't think I learned one person's name in sixty months.

There was only one conversation you really ever had to have in prison, with your fellow prisoners. General water cooler talk at a prison: "What are you in for?" "I killed my father." Every prisoner I met was very receptive to the idea of hating your father. "Why?" "He killed my mother." Without fail, the response to this, was some version of "Oh, good for you." Once word circulated that I was a nice man who liked to be left alone, and murdered his father for murdering his mother. Everything was fine. Everyone let me be. It was a wonderful place, and I missed it every day I was out.

I see my father in the distance, on the smoky path, wandering down from the mountain. He is coming at a faster pace than I am able to match. I am at the front of the line, just behind the woman with the seashell cut and I have been allowed to walk alone. I am the pace car. I am the insufferable slowness that I remember. I remember being forced to limp along, limp along, limp along. I am surprised to find that I am the reason why.

On the day I was released, I was given my personal effects and was told I had to check into whatever place every so many days. I had to pass drug tests. I never liked drugs, never trusted them, never understood the rules of them. How many is the right amount, how much is too much. The city of Philadelphia paid for a cab to take me anywhere within the city limits, and I went straight to a bar and stayed there.

I don't remember how, but I met a woman. I don't even like women very much, as women are a kind of person and people are not for me. I never bothered with relationships. I was drunk and she was drunk and we left and went somewhere and that was it.

Kayla. Her name was Kayla. Kayla had a boy in Jeanes Hospital in the Roxborough section of Northeast Philadelphia. I didn't find out for months. We didn't know each other at all, never did. I ran into her at the bar. And she broke into tears and said she had to confess something to me. Confess? I said. I laughed. Fuck you, I said. I laughed. It was midnight.

At 7 a.m. the next morning, I bought a greyhound ticket to Wilson, Arizona, a place I'd never heard of, and I never went back. Good luck Kayla. May you find your Edgar.

My father is in the distance again. The mountain has been extinguished and the smoke has cleared. His wounds have healed and he looks great. Like a young man. A spring in his automatic step. I am trudging along with my advanced age. I would like for it to be over. I am begging for it to end.

I found a trailer community in Arizona. Guys in prison said that the place to disappear was Alaska or Arizona. Alaska was gigantic, remote, and still occasionally got snow in the winter. It was full of ex-cons and people who never got caught or were looking to disappear, but I wanted the heat. Arizona was desolate wasteland getting increasingly hotter every day and I wanted that heat. I wanted to drink and sweat and look out across nothing and watch the end of the world start to boil the horizon.

I liked the idea that we were all near the end, it wasn't just me. I wasn't the only one not doing anything and letting myself waste away. I wanted to be there where the water had to be shipped in tanker trucks. I wanted to be on the vanguard of the end of the world, sleeping safe and sound with the air conditioner cranked all the way to high heaven. Freezing in a little trailer that was melting in the sun.

It was a double-wide. Very fancy. Used. Maybe twenty years old. It stunk. I didn't spend much time indoors apart from sleeping. I mostly sat outside in a plastic lawn chair and found my social streak with all these other lost souls hiding from the various past lives we had a shared disinterest of discussing.

I never felt any need to hide the fact that I was hiding from an accidental son, but nobody cared. I only had a few people suggest that I was doing the wrong thing, but the more they got to know me, the more they saw I was right. It was in his best interest. It is better to not be involved at all than to be too involved, to take over, to make my will his and force him into some life he doesn't want, all under the guise of "doing it for his sake." My mother tried to have the normal life and it killed her, my father needed a crutch to carry him through life, and I did my best to be that crutch until the very end. I would become a burden, or he would become a burden to me, we would feel the need to talk, to have birthdays and Christmases and it's better to sit here and be alone again among other people all doing their best to be alone. A whole community of people who don't want to be around other people. It wasn't much different from prison. Just so beautifully hot. 120° in the summer. 130° the following summer. Here it comes.

My father's figure is walking on the path against the stream, as he always has, but as he got close, and maybe there's still sand in my eyes, but it wasn't him. It looked like him. It looked like me. It looked like us. The figure was a smaller, gaunt version of myself. He looked hollow. He wasn't permitted to see me. I was permitted to see him. Tommy. Hello son, if you need me, I will be walking alone in the forest. I will be walking on the pine needles. I am always alone when there are pine needles. I almost made it this time. The mountain. I will never make it to the mountain.

I worked part-time in the Arizona heat, even though I swore I never would. I knew a guy who got me a job at a nearby store, keeping an eye on the parking lot overnight. A sixty-eight-year-old security guard, fading fast. I was not in the best health. I got an X-ray which featured a blurry area of concern in my lower abdomen, but I was not listening and found the process ridiculous. I got lost in the doctor's explanation and looked at my feet until he stopped talking. I started losing my focus, my concentration, I'd fade in and out of place. Nodding off in unlikely places, suddenly waking to find myself in bed, or my chair, or on the kitchen floor with a nosebleed.

The trailer was only nineteen feet long and I'd lose everything I set down. I kept leaving notes around the place to remind myself of things I forgot, but nothing worked. The smoke alarm chirped from the dead battery for weeks, every sixty seconds. Eek eek. Eek eek. Forever. If it saved the energy from the goddamn chirping, it'd last another year. Longer than me, probably. Between chirps, I'd forget the battery was dead, that I had to replace it. I'd begin again on the beeps. Oh right, the smoke alarm.

Eek eek. Oh right, the smoke alarm. Eek eek. Oh right, the smoke alarm.

I got a letter from Kayla about a year before, she'd tracked me down. "I wouldn't ask if I had a better idea. But Tommy. Our son." The letter went on to talk about Tommy's problems. She'd found him recently walking the wrong way down Frankford Avenue. Thirty-five years old. Dead-eyed, staring into the distance, completely unmoored from reality. He disappeared a lot over the years and she was unfortunately frozen in place, Tommy's problems kept her moored to Tommy as his mother, forever.

She didn't know what to do. She'd dragged him from place to place, getting help, spent the last of her money on the last of the interventions, and it was no use. He was there one minute swearing up and down that life would be different, and gone the next, disappeared for a week. In the middle of Pennsylvania August, which you don't want to be caught in, if you could help it. "He's probably living under a bridge by now. There's a place in Minnesota that I think would be good for him. It's a winter retreat. It's beautiful there that time of year. He can be outside and be with people his own age."

She'd gotten him a job at the bar when he was old enough to work and he never left. Spent most of his high school years there. Never graduated. Looked just like me from the pictures. I put one of the pictures on my fridge and lost track of the letter nearly instantly. Good luck, Tommy. Sorry I left before you got the chance to kill me. You really would have enjoyed it, I think.

My eyes blur and I have my body back. I am youngish

again. The pine needles are green. I relish the fluidity of every step. I feel the slick and easy movement of each joint, I focus on each and every part of myself, from my toes to the top of my immobile head. I relish each moment. What a glory it is to be wherever this is, in this perfectly wonderful body.

I must be taking the wrong lessons from this experience and I am suddenly lifted above the treeline and dropped, allowed to fall freely to the forest floor. I brace for impact but only my father hits and the light from the ambulance floods my field of vision. There is an EMT shaking me awake, from both shoulders, shoving me in the back of my seat, shaking me awake, she's dead, he says, shoving me into the frozen sand. Everything is blurring together all at once and I am dragged by the ankles through the forest, the pine needles digging into my back, the dirt flying above my face. I am the blade in the earth, I am creating space for new seeds, I am the eternal and endless forest, I am alone but for the pine needles, I am alone but these are mine, belong to me and enter the back of me, drag me where you will and the twisted tree of trees is breathing and heaving flames, protected by a yellow mosaic knight, and I am standing with my family in a clearing. We are all here. We are all finally together. Hello. Hello. Hello. Hello.

I die in a heap. I run out of whisky around 6 p.m. on a Sunday, like clockwork. Like I always did. I always run out of whisky on Sunday at 6. I like to go to the store around Sunday at 7. I like to ignore the pain in my side all week and drink just the same as I always did. I like to get back from the store and pour myself another drink over ice in the blazing hot Arizona sun and think back over my perfectly awful life. What a ridiculous life this has turned out to be. The booze turns into emotions and I allow myself to feel pure joy and pure sadness and pure relief and pure euphoria and the glass slips from my fingers and I never take another sip.

My father and I are playing catch on the beach. He'd driven us down to the shore directly after the funeral. We are throwing a baseball and we are having a heart to heart. He finally decides that it is time to talk to me, now, when I am nine and have just buried my mother and have never played catch before.

It is a rare moment of introspection that I never see in him again for as long as I live, and in the moment I know that it's important. I know that even with everything that is going on, with my mother, with death, trying to find a place for it all in my tiny little mind, I know on some level, it'd happened before and will happen again, that one of the most important moments of my life will be this stupid catch between two people who have never thrown or caught a baseball.

My father suddenly realized this fact after the burial. After the luncheon with her work friends. It turned out she had work friends and a woman from the neighbourhood she took walks with at night. We'd never met her before. She was beautiful and absolutely devastated. She worried over me and said that she was moving. She kept saying that she was moving. She was so sorry she hadn't stopped by to meet me, she said she would like to watch me grow up, but her husband had a new job in Colorado.

My father, after being shielded by me for hours, grabbed me by the shoulders and said, calmly, clearly. "We have never played catch. What the fuck am I doing?" He sped to a K-Mart after the funeral, the both of us in our pathetic suits, and we were going to go to the nearest field, but he wasn't paying attention and wound up on I-95, and he said "Fuck it. Let's go to the beach." And so we went.

We played catch a block and a half from where my mother died. Where there were still cones covering the spot, the road was fine, but somehow it seemed important to wait a certain amount of time before they let people park over the space. It was temporarily hallowed ground. It only lasted another week.

The ball was thrown by both parties in a high arc. Neither of us feeling terribly confident the other would catch it. I didn't have the strength or coordination for baseball, and I mostly threw it over his head and he'd have to run in his church shoes through the sand to go collect the ball. "I'm sorry," I said. Having to turn and chase the ball would interrupt his sermon, his long serious heart to heart that he really seemed to be putting a lot of effort into. A lot of thought. I couldn't hear him over the wind and the ocean, and the birds and the focus of catching a ball. I was too nervous to tell him. I just focused on the ball. I watched his mouth move and tears run down his face and was never so scared in my life.

When we were done he had a real smile. Maybe the only one I ever saw. The relief of having gotten all that off his chest. He came close enough to hug me, but didn't, he stalled at the last moment and instead put his hand on my shoulder and squatted down to tell me: "It's going to be okay. We just have to stick together. We can make it work."

Two weeks later he disappeared for three days. He was locked up in Buffalo, New York, about four hundred miles from home. His uncle, who I'd heard about, but never met, dropped him at the door. He came in to check things out, check up on me. Asked me what I'd been up to. "Nothing." Did you go to school? "No." No, he repeated. No, of course not, why would you.

My father didn't look at me and hurried upstairs. "I need a shower." His uncle, old, smelled like cigarettes, moved terrifyingly close to me, breaking the stranger barrier by a significant margin, close enough so that I could hear him whisper, even though my father had already closed the bathroom door and wouldn't have been interested to listen anyway. "He's always been like this. He'll always be like this. You look after yourself, and you call me if you need anything." He didn't leave his number and my father never spoke to him again, never spoke of him again. From previous stories, I know that his Uncle John bailed him out at least a half dozen times. From seventeen to that weekend. Uncle John was a saviour, "He should have been my father. Maybe he was, who knows?"

Health and human services made their first visit of many this weekend. It would be an ongoing visit for months and would happen every so often for the next several years. Before they arrived, we would have a team meeting and we would review my responses to likely questions. It was understood that I would be lying, encouraged. We were pulling the wool over their eyes. "Just say upbeat bullshit."

My son Tommy's loop went like this:

He was born to a single mother with a father who had run away from him. Not just left, but scattered at the very idea of him. Ran away in terror at the thought of having created another human being. He'd made his father live in Arizona. His father did not work for the Air Force as his mother had said. In the morning, most mornings, when he was sober enough to think, this was his first thought. His father. Just like his father. And his father before him.

Tommy lived in different places, was hard to track down, and mostly lived in the streets, under bridges, and for a long time, in a storage unit. In her letter, his mother wrote about how the storage unit wasn't so bad, it was abandoned, nobody was using it anyway. Tommy was a whiz and hooked up some lights. He had the run of the place and he got arrested for trespassing, but who cares.

Tommy did drugs until he fell asleep. When he ran out of drugs, he would steal from his mother, promise her things that would encourage her to give him more money, more things, make her look in the other direction while he stole her jewellery. He was going to go into the Air Force like his fake old man. It would set him straight. He would be fine. Everything would be fine.

Tommy would leave in the night, or get sober for a few days, and begin again.

I know some of this from Kayla's letter, and other things a father just knows.

In the clearing the tree is burning without heat, the knight is fidgety, bored. He picks his fingernails with the blade of his sword and scans the horizon for danger, or something more interesting to look at. We stand in a circle: my father, my mother, my son, and I. It would be awkward if we were able to move, but we can't. There is a sound in the distance like thunder that shakes the ground, and throws the trees into sway, sending pine needles in every direction. The knight tenses, then hangs his head and waits. It comes again. The pine needles spray. And again. The knight sets his sword down and clasps his hands in prayer. My family is non-responsive, dummies on strings, same as me, same as always.

A few days before I die, I receive word from Kayla that Tommy was found on the church stairs, maybe seeking sanctuary. Maybe he hadn't dealt with the church enough to know that they'd never open those doors. Not in a million years. It was January, it didn't get cold enough for him to freeze, but he died of exposure and everything else that was in his system. The letter from Kayla was accusatory, suggested it was my fault. And she was right, but not for the reasons she thought. He was doomed. Same as me. I drank to his memory, what little there was of it. I wished him well and made sure I didn't feel any way in particular about it. I tried to feel happy we never met, I think that our not having met probably gave him an extra five years, probably gave me an extra ten. What a gift to have never met.

There wasn't much to be done, this was the path that we were on. There is only the path, there is no other path, I am walking alone in the forest, same as Tommy. There are only so many chances to crawl out of the path, and you will miss them, you will be too stupid to recognize the off-ramps, you will be drunk, or angry or lost or alone. There are only so many chances and you will miss every single one. You will start over every day, and end up exactly where you began, only to fail again.

The trees part and the mountain is beyond, completely in flames. The light from the mountain mingles with the light from the tree and the knight shields his eyes and braces for the impact of the next step. It is staggering, if not held in place, I would scatter like the pines which are thrown, in all directions, breaking off, one after the other at the roots. My family screams and is reduced to dry earth, and they shatter into nothing, turning to mist in the shockwave.

I am alone. In a cavernous white room. With no tree. And no mountain. And no fire. And no knight. No pines. No needles. Alone. Finally alone.

There is a small voice, too close, that whispers in my ear. I am offered the opportunity to begin again.

I decline.

# # #

Dan Sanders is a writer of short fiction, essays and vending machine repair guides. His writing has appeared or is forthcoming in *Hobart, Split Lip Magazine, Okay Donkey, The Hong Kong Review* and wherever fine vending equipment is sold. Dan lives in Media, Pennsylvania and can be found online at dan-sanders.com.